THE MOVIE-TOWN MURDERS

Working undercover gives
FBI Art Crime Team agent Jason West
the illusion that he's safe
from his stalker, Dr. Jeremy Kyser.
Though film history and preservation
are not Jason's area of expertise,
he's intrigued by the case
of a well-connected
UCLA film studies professor
whose family believes
she may have been murdered
after discovering a legendary lost 1950s film noir.

Meanwhile, on the other side of the country,
BAU Chief Sam Kennedy
gets disturbing news:
the Roadside Ripper, the serial killer
Sam believes murdered his college boyfriend,
may not have been working alone.

The Movie-Town Murders

Art of Murder Book V

Josh Lanyon

VELLICHOR BOOKS

An imprint of JustJoshin Publishing, Inc.

The Movie-Town Murders

The Art of Murder Book V

June 2022

Copyright (c) 2022 by Josh Lanyon

Cover by Johanna Ollila

Book designed by Kevin Burton Smith.

Editing by Keren Reed

ISBN: 978-1-945802-79-9

Published in the United States of America
JustJoshin Publishing, Inc.
3053 Rancho Vista Blvd.
Suite 116
Palmdale, CA 93551
www.joshlanyon.com

This is a work of fiction. Any resemblance to persons living or dead is entirely coincidental.

To the Divine Ms. M. The bravest gal I know.

If you want a happy ending, that depends, of course, on where you stop your story.

- Orson Welles

Author's Note

Dear Reader,

Some of the events referred to in ***The Movie-Town Murders*** actually take place in a coda for ***The Monuments Men Murders***, written as an exclusive for my Patreon group.

You may find it useful to listen to the audio of that coda, narrated by the wonderful Kale Williams, which is available at https://bit.ly/3zqCrbQ

CHAPTER ONE

He was halfway through the meeting with Kapszukiewicz before it dawned on him—he was not going to be fired.

Special Agent Jason West of the FBI's Art Crime Team was so flabbergasted, he actually missed the next few words of the chief of the Major Theft Unit of the Criminal Investigative Division, which oversaw ACT.

"Do you see the irony here?" Kapszukiewicz said.

Jason clipped out, "Yes, ma'am."

Yes. He did indeed see the bitter irony. Would Sam see the irony?

"For the record, I've never subscribed to the idea that everyone gets one mistake."

Jason half swallowed his husky, "No, ma'am."

"You're getting a second chance, West, because, with one exception, your performance over the past six years has been exemplary. You've earned the right to one mistake. One. *One* mistake. This was it. Any other agent under my command would be leaving this meeting without his badge and weapon."

"Understood." He drew a sharp breath. "And again, I'm very s—"

"I don't want to hear it." Kapszukiewicz's normally warm blue gaze was glacial. "The consensus is there were sufficient mitigating factors in this case. I concur. Don't prove me wrong. *Don't* fuck this up."

Seven minutes later Jason walked out of the private elevator, past the security cameras, the reception desk, the guard desk, the giant blue and gold FBI seal positioned between two flags (one for the good old US of A and the other the FBI's own standard) and the metal detectors of the security checkpoint. He pushed through the bulletproof glass door, leaving the official air-conditioned quiet for the hot, noisy sidewalk of Pennsylvania Avenue on a July afternoon.

It was almost disorienting to find himself back in the real world—and still employed. The summer air smelled of car exhaust, hot cement, and close calls.

He pocketed the lanyard with his ID, strode along the buff-colored concrete exterior with its repetitive, square, bronze-tinted windows set deep in black frames. Much like its namesake, the J. Edgar Building was not a handsome structure. In fact, that particular architectural style was known as Brutalist. Talk about *on the nose.*

Jason hailed the first available cab and jumped inside.

"DoubleTree Crystal City."

The cab, which had barely come to a stop, sped up again, slipping seamlessly into the flow of anonymous traffic, just another fish swimming upstream.

Jason dropped back in his seat, wiped his damp forehead on his sleeve, loosened his tie, and pulled out his cell. He thumbed Sam's number.

Sam picked up on the second ring. "Where are you?"

"Headed for the airport. Well, the DoubleTree. But it's okay. I'm okay. I'm still on the payroll. I'm not even on the beach." An hour ago, he'd been convinced suspension without pay or maybe ISL—Involuntary Stress Leave—would be his best-case scenario. He'd have counted himself lucky to receive either. *This* was almost more than he could take in.

Sam said crisply, "I'll meet you in the Skydome Lounge."

"You'll… You're still in DC?"

"Correct."

Though they'd flown together from LA to DC, Sam was supposed to be driving on to Quantico and then eventually to his home in Stafford.

Jason held his phone away and studied it doubtfully. Putting it to his ear once more, he said ruefully, "You must have thought I was finished for sure."

"No. I figured Kapszukiewicz was too smart to throw the baby out with the bathwater, but you can't always predict."

"*I* thought I'd be bounced." No lie. Jason had walked into that meeting with the cheery confidence of a man facing a firing squad.

Even at that reduced volume, Sam's sardonic, "You're the agent who found a long-lost Vermeer, West," came through loud and clear. "Firing you would look terrible on TV."

Ouch.

But that was partly what Kapszukiewicz had been referring to by "consensus." Far from wanting Jason's head on a platter, the LA Field Office's Special Agent in Charge Robert Wheat had been raising hell over Salt Lake City's Art Crime Team's "attempt to steal credit" for Jason's—to put it politely—

"black op." Wheat hadn't gone so far as to pretend he'd *sanctioned* Jason's actions, but he'd come close. Wheat was an ambitious guy, and he was hell-bent on the LA Office—and himself—getting credit for one of the biggest art recoveries of the past decade.

"Yeah, well."

"We'll talk when you get here." Sam clicked off.

Jason sank back and mopped his forehead again.

The Skydome Lounge was a revolving restaurant and bar on the top floor of the North Tower of the DoubleTree Hilton in Crystal City. The muted George Jetson meets George Washington decor was uninspired, but no one came for the beige ambiance or even the Tomahawk Ribeye. It took less than forty-five minutes for the glass dome to complete a full 360° rotation, and when the weather was clear, like today, the views of the Pentagon, DC, and the Potomac were phenomenal.

Also, the Skydome's bartenders understood the art of the free pour.

Jason scanned the mostly empty room and spotted Sam seated at a table beside the wall of windows. His dark suit jacket was draped on the back of the chair, and he was working on his laptop. For a moment Jason let himself enjoy the sight of Sam being Sam: his hard not-quite-handsome profile absorbed in whatever he was reading, white shirtsleeves rolled to reveal tanned, muscular forearms, one well-shod foot moving in absent, restless rhythm.

At a nearby table, two attractive, well-dressed women whispered to each other and tittered as they sized Sam up.

Otherwise, the restaurant was deserted. A DJ station sat vacant in the middle of the room, surrounded by a small parquet dance floor that would barely accommodate three couples. Four large televisions tuned to MSNBC hung from the ceiling, reporting on the continued lack of cooperation from pretty much everyone for pretty much everything.

As Jason approached, Sam glanced up. His severe expression softened, though in order to recognize that, you'd have to know what to look for. Sam took off his gold-wire glasses and pushed down the lid of his laptop.

Jason said, "Hey." He was still disconcerted—though happy, no question—to find Sam waiting for him in his hotel.

"Hi." Sam studied him. "Okay?"

Jason nodded, pulled out the chair across from Sam, and sat down. "Yep. Just…surprised."

About everything. The truth was, he felt shaken in the aftermath of all that adrenaline. The way you did after any close call. He'd been braced for the worst. He was still trying to absorb that the worst hadn't come to pass.

Sam nodded to the bartender, who crossed the little dance floor to them. "What are you drinking?" Sam asked Jason.

"Whatever's on tap," Jason told the bartender.

She nodded. Glanced at the empty rocks glass next to Sam's elbow. "Another?"

Sam nodded. As the bartender walked away, he said to Jason, "What happened?"

Jason said cautiously, "Kapszukiewicz said you phoned her?"

"We talked on Friday. She hadn't come to a decision yet."

Jason offered Sam a crooked smile. "Then you'll appreciate the irony. Per Kapszukiewicz, both my grandfather and Roy Thompson are deceased and therefore have—had—no active ongoing 'interest' in the case."

Sam's brow furrowed as he processed.

"Had Thompson still been alive and facing prosecution, the possibility that my grandfather allegedly ordered him to steal artifacts could have created conflict on my part, since my grandfather could, again allegedly, have been materially involved in the conduct subject to my investigation."

Jason could see the moment it clicked. Sam's eyes—the same uncompromising blue of the FBI seal—flickered. His mouth curved wryly. "Your investigation was into ownership of the art, not whether Thompson was guilty of theft."

"Yes. Right." Jason expelled a long breath. "Whether my grandfather ordered Thompson to take the art and other items—which he'd never have done—or Thompson 'liberated' those things on his own, the bottom line is the treasure was still stolen."

Sam looked thoughtful. "How the art was acquired wouldn't affect the outcome of the investigation."

Jason laughed, wiped his eyes because this was still painful. "Right. In a nutshell. Which is what I must have been. Nuts. What concerns Kapszukiewicz isn't the ethical conflict. It's that *I* believed there was an ethical conflict—and acted accordingly."

Sam said, "It's always the cover-up, never the crime." He added, "Not that you committed or would commit any crime."

Jason appreciated that Sam felt that way now. He hadn't seemed to feel that way three days ago.

"Right. I just…short-circuited. I don't know why."

"I do," Sam was curt. "You do too. So does Kapszukiewicz." Sam had made no bones about the fact that he believed Jason was suffering from nervous exhaustion. He'd probably shared that belief with Kapszukiewicz. Which Jason did not appreciate, but, given recent events, could hardly argue with.

Sam must have been reviewing his own actions and reactions because he added, "This is why speaking to an ethics official *ahead* of time would be helpful."

"Yes. Agreed."

Sam had viewed Jason's actions as negatively as Jason had. It was never going to be funny, but it *was* a lesson to both of them. About a number of things.

Jason flicked him a rueful look. "So when you phoned Kapszukiewicz on Friday, that was before you left Montana?"

Sam's pale brows rose in polite inquiry.

"Before you arrived in LA. Before we talked." The hours during which Jason had believed their relationship truly was over. And, he would have bet, the hours during which Sam had also believed their relationship was at an end. Because he had ended it.

Or at least that had been Jason's takeaway because then, like now, Sam had said nothing.

And continued to say nothing.

"Thank you." Jason steadied his voice. "I mean it. You didn't have to do that. Especially given your feelings about… everything."

"I shared my thoughts with Kapszukiewicz. But I can't tell another unit chief how to handle their team. I wouldn't if I could."

"No, I know." And yet, per Kapszukiewicz, Sam *had*, in his own way, interceded on Jason's behalf. That alone had shaken Jason. It was like discovering the sun could occasionally, when it chose, rise in the west and set in the east.

They had traveled a very long distance since that final confrontation in Sam's temporary office at the Bozwin RA. A distance that had nothing to do with the thousand-plus miles between Montana and California. In fact, most of the journey had happened over the weekend in Jason's little bungalow on Carroll Canal.

"Personal feelings aside, you're a good agent, West. You're ACT's superstar. I think firing you would be a huge miscalculation. For a lot of reasons." Jason opened his mouth, but Sam added, "And as far as my personal feelings?" He gave a funny smile. "I think you know there's not much I wouldn't do for you."

Jason really didn't want to get caught crying in his beer—especially when the beer had yet to arrive. He said briskly, "George phoned too, also asking for clemency." He was trying to joke, but mild-mannered Supervisory Special Agent George Potts's attempt to save him meant nearly as much as Sam's.

The bartender arrived then with their drinks. It seemed Sam was running a tab. So was he not heading out to Quantico after all?

Jason picked up his frosted beer mug. Sam lightly knocked the heel of his glass to Jason's. "Welcome back, West."

Jason dipped his head in acknowledgment—the weirdest things choked him up lately. "Geronimo." He took a long swallow of beer.

"Anyway, like I said, you're a valuable asset." Sam sipped his drink. Yet when his gaze met Jason's, there was a look that got to Jason in some hard to explain way. Not sympathy exactly, but a sort of utter and complete understanding that gave Jason a peculiar feeling in his belly, left him feeling warm and weak.

Maybe—well, no maybe about it—it *wasn't* fair or even accurate, but he'd always believed there were conditions attached to Sam's...affection for him. Now they seemed to have crossed into a no man's land of awareness and acceptance. He had no idea what their future held, but he felt confident of Sam's feelings in a way he never really, fully had before.

Jason sipped his beer, watching a plane flying into Regan International. In a few hours he'd be flying out himself. But he was not going to look beyond this minute, this stolen time with Sam. God only knew when they'd be in the same town at the same time again.

Suddenly, he remembered something from the interview in Kapszukiewicz's office and made a sound of amusement.

"What?" Sam asked.

"I almost forgot. Kapszukiewicz said J.J. phoned and told her he objected to having three different partners during his field training period and would prefer that I remain at the LA Field Office."

Sam choked on his whiskey sour. "Jesus Christ." He hastily wiped his chin.

Jason laughed.

They had a couple more drinks, talked about nothing much. Jason's thoughts kept pinging back to the meeting with Kapszukiewicz, reliving every excruciating minute. He was torn between abject relief he still had a career, and mortification that he had come so close to losing it.

By the time five o'clock rolled around, the bar was filling up, the noise level rising accordingly.

Sam raised his brows. "Did you want to order dinner or…?"

Jason's heart lifted. That was one question answered. Sam was staying over. He smiled. "Or. Definitely or."

Sam's mouth quirked. He pushed his chair back.

Chapter Two

The elevator was crowded.

This was Washington DC, and the hotel was full of government employees. Sam and Jason stood silent, shoulders pressed against each other, hands occasionally, furtively brushing, as they slowly returned earthward. Floor by floor, they patiently waited each time the elevator lurched to a stop, doors sliding open, people crowding in, people crowding out, doors sliding closed.

Each time the elevator doors dinged, Jason prayed they didn't run into someone they—or more likely Sam—knew.

Not because they were violating any rules. The Bureau did not have a non-fraternization policy for employees. But because running into someone they knew would mean delay.

Seven slow-motion stops before they reached Jason's floor.

At last, they stepped into the hallway with its iron sconces and crimson-olive-gold pseudo art deco carpet. The air smelled of cleaning supplies and pleasant, strategically diffused citrusy scent. The muted light threw a greenish cast over everything, including Sam and Jason. They exchanged quick, slightly self-conscious smiles.

The elevator doors closed behind them, and less than a minute later they were finally alone.

Jason's room offered still more panoramic views of the now twinkling Washington DC skyline: the Washington Monument, Jefferson Memorial, Lincoln Memorial, and, of course, the White House, iconic silhouettes against the sunset. There was the usual functional work desk, flat-screen TV, and, crucially, a fairly comfortable king-size bed.

The bed being the actual only point of interest.

Jason tossed his keycard onto the desk, unclipped his pistol, and laid that aside as well. Sam flipped the deadbolt on the door, tossed his briefcase and jacket onto a corner chair. He loosened his tie as he moved to the bed, tossed his tie onto the pile of jacket and briefcase. He laid his weapon on the bed stand.

By then Jason was out of his shirt and trousers. He smiled, reaching for Sam, unfastening his shirt buttons with the speed of practice. Sam nuzzled the curve of Jason's neck, hands going to his own trousers' fastening. Jason shoved Sam's crisp white shirt off his shoulders and kissed the fierce jut of Sam's jaw.

"Not that I'm complaining, but why *did* you stay over?"

Sam stepped out of his trousers, arms circling Jason's waist, pulling him close. "WWWD." Sam's smile was mocking, but the mockery seemed to be directed at himself.

"World Wide Wrestling Day?"

"What Would West Do."

"What would…" Jason laughed. True enough. If he'd thought Sam needed his support, he'd say to hell with everything else and be there for him. But it was hard to imagine Sam ever needing his support, not in any significant way, and

Sam had warned him early on not to look for, well, too much. Granted, Sam had proven himself wrong numerous times on that one. Even in Montana, as angry and disgusted as he'd been—and with the future of their relationship in serious doubt—he'd tried to intercede on Jason's behalf. And that meant everything.

"You're a nice guy, Kennedy," Jason said gravely.

Sam's mouth twitched in a half-smile. "I know."

"I don't care what anybody says."

Sam laughed. "Yeah, well, neither do I." And that was absolutely the truth.

But yes, Jason was happy about anything that delayed their inevitable goodbyes. This goodbye would not be nearly as crushing as their goodbye in Montana, though, and he was grateful for that.

They stretched out on the bed, holding each other, gazing into each other's eyes. In the elevator, Jason had felt this moment would never come, but now that it was here, now that they were once more in each other's arms, he felt that he wanted to savor every second.

Sam too seemed in no hurry, kissing him in soft, slow nuzzles, gentle kisses, cherishing kisses.

The unexpected sweetness of stolen kisses on a workday afternoon.

Technically, it was evening now. Through the large windows, Jason could see clouds gilded rose gold by the sunset.

He said dreamily, "Kapszukiewicz even assigned me a new case."

"Did she?" Sam raised his head, his breath warm against Jason's face. "What's the case?"

"Undercover gig at UCLA."

Sam cocked an eyebrow. "Undercover. You'll enjoy that."

Jason agreed, though at this point he'd have gratefully accepted stakeout in Siberia.

"The Bureau is doing a solid for a former California senator. Francis Ono."

"Francis Ono? That's a blast from the past."

"Literally. He was one of the big proponents of nuclear energy, back in the day. Old-school conservative, for sure. Which is why it was a big deal when he endorsed Clark's reelection campaign."

Clark Vincent was an ambitious Republican congressman married to Jason's sister Sophie. In fact, Sophie would be hurt if she knew Jason was in DC but choosing to spend the night in a hotel rather than her home. As much as he loved his sister, Jason detested Clark and strenuously avoided spending even a minute more in his company than he had to.

"So you're acquainted with Ono?"

"Me? No. I've never met him. His granddaughter was a film studies professor. She died six months ago in what LAPD deemed accident-possible-suicide. The family insists there's no way."

Sam said wearily, "The family usually does. Cause of death?"

"Autoerotic asphyxiation."

"Fun stuff."

So true. Deliberately strangling yourself while attempting to heighten the sexual experience was not the most dignified exit.

"It could have been an accident, but the senator is convinced his granddaughter was murdered."

"And why would anyone want to take out a film studies professor?"

"I guess that's what I'll find out. I haven't seen the case file yet."

Sam seemed to mull it over. "UCLA. That's your old alma mater, isn't it?"

"Mm-hm."

"And where that cute little art professor your sister Charlotte tried to set you up with teaches?" Sam's tone was dry.

"I have zero interest in art professors, cute or otherwise." Which was true. Jason was surprised Sam even remembered Alexander Dash. They'd met very briefly at Jason's birthday party in February.

Sam's mouth curved. "Good. Keep your eye on the ball, West."

Jason said slyly, "Which ball would you prefer, Kennedy?"

Sam laughed, hooked a muscular arm beneath Jason's waist, and rolled him over so that they were eye to eye, nose to nose, mouth to mouth.

"Hello again," Jason said.

Sam's mouth twitched. "Hi."

"Thanks for sticking around today. Seriously."

"No thanks needed." Sam lifted his head, his mouth latched on to Jason's, and he kissed him with cool competency. Jason smiled, opened his mouth to the probe of Sam's tongue.

Sam kissed him again, and that kiss was less considered and a lot more heated.

Jason gasped, like Sleeping Beauty startled back to life, and kissed him back. The weird sense of distance, of detachment he'd felt since walking out of Kapszukiewicz's office fell away. Sam's hands swept through his hair, holding Jason to kiss him more deeply, and Jason felt that caress to the ends of his hair, to the soles of his feet, like grabbing onto a live wire.

"I love you," Jason whispered, and felt Sam swallow the words, absorb the words.

The lovely wonder of this because by rights Sam should be miles away, well out of reach, and instead here he was, hands moving knowingly over Jason's body, warm, so warm on the thin skin of Jason's waist, ribs, that Jason would not have been surprised to catch fire, skin alight like tissue paper. Sam's fingertips grazing Jason's nipples, thumbnails flicking the sensitive tips.

Jason bit his lip to stop the moans of pleasure threatening to tear out of his throat—vaguely conscious of all the potential government employees staying at the DoubleTree—but his good intentions were lost as Sam's hand locked on the waistband of Jason's boxers, dragged them down, and took firm hold of Jason's cock.

Jason cried out, arched his hips in, distantly aware of the mattress sinking as Sam shifted position, lowered his head, and took the head of Jason's cock into the sweet warmth of his mouth.

"Jesus, Sam. That's so… *God.* That's so good…"

Understatement. That slow, strong suck into wet heat. Deep, deeper… His cock pulsing down Sam's throat—and that was no small part of the turn-on—the delicious craziness of *Sam Kennedy* performing this wrenchingly intimate act on him, for him.

Sam took his time.

"Going to come," Jason warned, though the neighbors—and possibly passengers boarding their flights over at National—had already figured it out.

Sam's response was to half swallow him.

Jason's vision seemed to incandesce, his heels dug into the bedding, and he convulsed with wave after wave of shivering, shimmering orgasm. Blood-hot salt shot out in wet spurts, and Sam swallowed, which nearly made Jason orgasm a second time. Not merely because of the raw sensuality of the act, the all-encompassing acceptance, which meant so much after the pain and misunderstanding of the previous week.

It was weird how much sleep he still needed.

Although this drowsing after sex was nothing to how much he'd slept over the long weekend. Then, even the knowledge that Sam was working in the next room or outside watering the garden or cooking dinner in the kitchen had not been enough to snap Jason from that almost drugged state of inertia. The constant, desperate need for sleep had dragged him down like a weighted blanket. So maybe Sam was right about the nervous exhaustion.

In which case, Jason could thank Sam for seeing him through that too.

Anyway, when he woke, a lamp in the corner was on, shade tilted down, and Sam was in bed beside him, reading over a case file.

At Jason's movement, Sam glanced over and smiled faintly.

"Good sleep?"

"It's not the company, I promise."

"I know." Sam took his glasses off, set the file on the floor.

Jason scooted closer, and Sam pulled him comfortably into his arms. Jason pillowed his head on Sam's chest, listening to the strong, steady beat of Sam's heart.

After a time, he said, "I asked Kapszukiewicz for a week's leave."

He felt Sam's surprise, though Sam only offered a non-committal, "Did you?"

"I'm overdue vacation anyway, so she agreed."

Sam said slowly, "Taking some time off is a good idea."

"I want to go see Hans de Haan's girlfriend, Anna."

Sam took a moment to answer. "That's not taking time off, though. That's still the job."

Sam's tone was neutral, but Jason could tell he didn't like the idea. Which Jason had guessed would be the case.

"It's not the only reason I want to go. I'd like to see the Netherlands, particularly where that Vermeer came from. But I do feel I owe it to de Haan."

Also, though he would not admit it aloud, the idea of being out of the country for a while, safely out of Dr. Jeremy Kyser's reach, definitely had its appeal.

"De Haan made his choices."

"Okay, *owe* is the wrong word. I just feel like someone should talk to her about what was going on with de Haan. What he was thinking."

Sam said quietly, bleakly, "Take it from me, these things rarely go the way you hope."

Jason raised his head, studied Sam's face. "I don't have any hopes. I just want her to know Hans had every intention of keeping his promise to marry her and have a child."

"You don't think she knows that?"

"She probably does. They were together a long time. But if something happened to you, I'd want to know you had been talking about me, thinking of me."

Sam said curtly, "You can take it for granted that I was thinking of you."

Jason gave a short laugh. "Okay. Well, thanks. I'll keep that in mind. And ditto. But some people might need a little more. I think Hans would want some effort made."

Sam sighed. "You're too sentimental, West."

Jason lifted a shoulder in a half-shrug, casually traced a finger between the flat, muscular planes of Sam's pecs, trailing gently down—smiling privately as Sam sucked in his stomach—feeling the silky, sparse hair, the smooth skin of Sam's cock pushing up to meet him.

Sam groaned softly and shifted on top of Jason, trapping their erections together.

Jason's breathing quickened, his hips lifting to meet Sam's down-thrust, jab, thrust, parry before they found their rhythm, gazes pinned to each other's faces. Eyes never wavering, naked in a way that had nothing to do with clothes. Jason raised his knees, ready, willing, if that's what Sam wanted, but Sam folded him close, legs entwined, and they thrust together, faster, faster.

Sam held Jason so tight, he wondered if he'd crack a rib, and their rhythm soared to a pounding.

Sam ground out, "Christ, West," and began to come in volcanic bursts of sticky, hot wet.

Jason's orgasm seemed to swell from the base of his spine, exploding seconds later.

Neither moved when it was over. They lay pressed against each other, dazedly watching the languorous roll and tumble of stars and silvery clouds moving through the night sky.

The second time Jason woke, it was to the annoying *buzz* of a cell phone.

He clawed his way back to the surface, fumbling for his phone, aware of Sam on his right, doing the same.

"It's me," Sam said over his shoulder, and Jason gratefully fell face-first back into the pillows. He closed his eyes, willing himself to unconsciousness, but try as he might, he couldn't quite slide back into sleep, couldn't quite tune out Sam's side of the conversation.

"No. Go ahead."

Silence.

No, not silence, because Jason could hear that little *zizz* on the other end of the line, like an electrical short right before fire broke out.

Sam swore softly, and the mattress dipped as he rose and moved across the floor to the window. Jason lifted his head. He could make out Sam's silhouette in front of the picture window. Phone to his ear, Sam seemed to be gazing down at Jefferson

Memorial. He kept his voice low so as to not disturb Jason, but really that just made it all the easier to hear the tiny female *buzz* on the other end of the conversation. That would be Jonnie. In her brief stint in the BAU, Special Agent Jonnie Gould had quickly made herself all but indispensable to her chief.

Which said something for Jonnie, given that Jason couldn't think of another human Sam considered indispensable.

"Okay. Get me on the first available flight out of National."

The pocket-sized voice on the other end of the call began to protest.

Sam cut her off. "You can meet with the Executive Assistant Director. It'll be a good experience for you."

The protests grew louder. Sam said crisply, "It's decided," and disconnected.

Jason whistled soundlessly.

Sam returned to bed. The mattress dipped beneath his weight. They moved back into each other's arms, and Jason murmured, "Serve you right if Jonnie quits."

"She's not going to quit," Sam said. "She lives for this job."

Yeah. No. She really didn't. No one on Sam's team lived for the job but Sam.

Jason tipped his head back to study Sam's profile in the gloom. "Where are you headed?"

"Idaho."

Idaho was not on Sam's regular itinerary. Jason thought it over. "Cowboy Ike." He identified one of Sam's final cases as a field agent before his promotion to BAU chief. "What's wrong with the case?"

"Political infighting between the mayor and the state attorney's office."

"What? How can—"

"Witness recantation."

"Hell."

"A steep decline in the quality of basic police work."

Uh-oh. Jason had heard this speech before.

"What do you think you can accomplish by flying out there now?"

Sam said grimly, "We'll soon find out." He let out a long, impatient breath, absently stroking Jason's hair. "Anyway, we've still got about two hours before we need to get moving."

Jason nodded, closed his eyes. For a few moments they breathed in quiet unison.

They had spent most of the last four days together, and even though Jason had slept through a good portion of the weekend, Sam's presence in the little house on the canal had been a reassuring constant. The realization that it would probably be weeks before they saw each other again was a near physical ache. A weight on his chest that made it hard to draw a full breath.

Not that it was anything new for them. The only real change was, after the events of the past week, Jason understood that the separation was difficult for Sam too.

Jason said, "The goodbyes are getting harder."

"Yes," Sam said.

CHAPTER THREE

Home sweet home.

Jason stuck his key in the side door lock of the little blue house. Summer sounds drifted from the canal behind the house: the quacking of ducks, the splash and paddle of little boats, laughter. Warmth radiated from the brick walkway, and the sweet honey smell of the bougainvillea covering the pergola filled the air.

He was very glad to be home, but it had been a good trip. The Netherlands—Delft, in particular—had been beautiful, enchanting. Like Venice, Delft was bordered by canals, but unlike Venice, Delft was a city of ancient architecture, medieval gardens, and churches that actually felt hallowed. Anyway, he didn't mind travel—it was part of the job—but there was something to be said for home and hearth and a really good mattress.

He'd been living in the quirky but charming 1924 bungalow on Carroll Canal for just about two years. It was his first real home, and he loved everything about it: the blue shake siding, angled rooms, sloping ceilings, all the windows offering picturesque views of the canal, and the small but luxurious garden that led right down to the water. A wall of bamboo and tropical banana palms created a tall hedge, though it was only useful from the ground up. The new multistory homes towering on either side of the cottage had a perfect view right into Jason's backyard.

He turned the key in the lock, pushed open the door, and jumped back as someone charged around the corner of the house, shouting, "You! Halt!"

A stocky middle-aged man in a blue security-guard uniform pointed a semiautomatic at Jason's chest.

"Hands up!"

Jason let go of his suitcase handle, raised his hands, and, over the hop, skip, and jump of his heart, demanded, "Who the hell are you?"

The security guard's beady gaze was veering from Jason's suitcase to his expression and back again. "You're Jason? Let's see some ID."

"Are you kidding me? Who *are* you?"

"ID. *Slowly.*"

Swearing quietly, Jason reached into his jeans pocket and slowly withdrew his passport. He flipped it open, held it up.

The guard studied it, nodded at last, holstered his weapon, and said, "Sorry about that, Jason. I didn't recognize you with the beard. We weren't expecting you back until tonight."

Jason shoved his passport in his pocket. "*We?* Who's we? Who are *you*?"

"Horace Pratt. Your family hired me to watch this property."

"You're fired."

Horace looked slightly—only slightly—apologetic. "The thing is, you're not my employer. You can't actually fire m—"

"Get off my property."

Once again, Horace seemed mildly apologetic and mostly unfazed. "Okay. You're upset. But you might want to phone Mrs. Baldwin."

Mrs. Baldwin, AKA Charlotte, was Jason's eldest sister.

"You're damned right I'm phoning her. Get your gear together."

Jason retrieved his suitcase, lifted it over the doorstop, and slammed shut the kitchen door. Through the kitchen window he watched Horace turn and disappear around the back of the house.

Jason expelled an exasperated breath and phoned Charlotte at Le Cottage Bleu, the vintage home boutique shop she owned.

Charlotte greeted him with a cheery, "Hey there! How was your trip? Did you go to a lot of museums?"

"Fine. Yes. Did you hire a security guard to watch my house?"

"Oh good, you've met Horace."

"*Not* good. Horace pulled his weapon on me. I don't like people who point pistols at me."

"Oh dear. Of course not," Charlotte soothed. "No one does. But now that Horace knows you, it won't happen again."

"No, it won't. Because I've fired him."

This seemed to amuse his sister mightily. "You can't fire him. You didn't hire him."

"I can sure as hell forbid him access to my property!"

She sighed. "Yes, you can, and it will make his job more difficult."

Jason struggled for patience. He knew she meant well. They all—his family—meant well. "Charlie, I don't want or need a bodyguard—"

"He's not. He's a security guard."

"I don't want or need a security guard! For God's sake. I'm an FBI agent. This is ridiculous!"

"Listen, there's nothing to be embarrassed about."

"I didn't say I was embarrassed. I said—"

"I talked it over with Daddy, and we're agreed that having someone there to keep an eye on the house is the ideal solution. It'll give you a little peace of mind. And it'll give *us* a little peace of mind."

"I appreciate your concern, but no. *No.*" Phone balanced precariously between cheek and shoulder, he unzipped his suitcase and began pulling clothes out to do his laundry. He had an appointment with former senator Francis Ono in a couple of hours, after which he was supposed to take up residence in Georgette Ono's former apartment on Wilshire Blvd. and prepare for Monday's classes.

It was a little over a week since his meeting with the chief of the Major Theft Unit of the Criminal Investigative Division, and her warning not to screw up again was still ringing in his ears.

Meanwhile Charlotte was still coaxing and cajoling. "Anyway, it's not forever. Just until this situation with the mad doctor is resolved. You have to be able to relax sometimes."

"I was perfectly relaxed until your rent-a-cop pulled a gun on me."

Charlotte said sweetly, "You don't *sound* very relaxed."

"Because I just had a Colt semiautomatic aimed at my chest! Anyway, it's not necessary. I'm not even going to be here while I'm working this case."

"Then it doesn't do any harm to have Horace there, does it? It's not as though we're asking you to pay his salary. This is our *gift* to you. A gift we're also giving to ourselves so we don't have to *worry* so much about you. Think of Dad. Think of the Duchess. The constant worry is so hard on them."

The Duchess was Charlie's nickname for their somewhat formidable mother, Ariadne Harley-West. A woman whose superpower was complete immunity to worry, constant or otherwise.

"Oh boy. Turn the screws a little tighter, why don't you?" Jason continued to argue as he emptied his bags and sorted through what he'd need over the coming week. The problem was, he didn't have infinite time to spend squabbling with his overprotective family. He had a laundry list of things he needed to get done, including, yes, laundry.

He bundled his dirty clothes and carried them to the washing machine in the little back porch. "Fine," he said at last, curtly, peeling off his T-shirt and tossing that too into the washer. He slammed shut the lid. "But Horace needs to be gone when I get back."

"*Of course,*" Charlie soothed. "Of course, we can talk about it then."

While Jason's laundry ran through the washer cycles, he made himself a slightly stale cheese and pickle sandwich and phoned his partner, Special Agent J.J. Russell. Russell would be working the Ono case from the LA Field Office while Jason pursued the investigation on-site at UCLA.

"Yo. You're back. It's about time."

Jason snorted. "I missed you too, Russell."

"Yeah, but seriously. What a time to take a vacation."

"It wasn't exactly a vacation."

Russell sighed. "Right. How was Holland? How was de Haan's girlfriend?"

"Holland is beautiful. Crooked houses. Cobblestone streets. Canals and courtyards and coffeehouses." Jason stared out the window at Horace, who had wandered down the stone steps to stare into the canal. What the hell was he doing down there? Fishing? "The girlfriend is heartbroken."

"Yeah, well. De Haan should have thought of her before he went breaking and entering in the dark of night."

Not exactly the warm and fuzzy type, Russell, although Jason wasn't going to forget Russell had—in his own way—stood up for him.

"Well, we all make mistakes."

"Tell me about it," Russell said grimly. "Speaking of which, now that you're back maybe you can let Shane Donovan know we do *occasionally* handle non-art-related cases."

Special Agent Shane Donovan was Jason's Northern California counterpart. Despite the fact that illegal activity in the high-end art market left the $50 billion industry vulnerable to numerous financial abuses, including money laundering and funding terrorism, there were still only twenty-five full-time agents on the entire Art Crime Team. The DOJ's official view was that regulatory issues needed to remain the Bureau's higher priority. Russell, for example, though partnered with Jason, was not technically a full-time member of the Art Crime Team.

"What's up with Donovan?"

"Don't get excited. Nothing to do with Fletcher-Durrand."

Jason's rocketing hopes fizzled. "Damn."

The disintegration five months earlier of the case Jason and Shane had painstakingly built against the Fletcher-Durrand art gallery still stung. Jason had put his heart and soul into constructing a prosecutable case of fraud, grand larceny, and forgery, only to see the result of all that effort melt away like a sand castle at high tide.

Worse, one Durrand brother, if not both, was implicated in a series of gruesome torture slayings spanning decades, culminating in the death of a Los Angeles reporter. Their prime suspect, Shepherd Durrand, had fled to France on a one-way ticket before he could be arrested and officially charged.

J.J. added, "Though I've got to say, I still don't see how *this* case falls under the Bureau's purview. I don't see how it's even a case. If the family's unhappy with the conclusion of the police investigation, they should hire a private investigator."

Jason quoted, *"The FBI may engage in undercover activities and undercover operations that are appropriate to carry out its law enforcement responsibilities, including the conduct of preliminary inquiries, general crimes investigations, and criminal intelligence investigations."*

"George already read me the Attorney General's Guidelines, AKA the riot act."

"In preliminary inquiries, these methods may be used to further the objective of inquiry into possible criminal activities by individuals or groups to determine whether a full investigation is warranted."

"Did you memorize that on the flight? I'm just saying, I don't see the point. There was *already* a full investigation. Did you look over the files I sent?"

"I'm still going through everything. But that reminds me. Can we get one of our own forensic pathologists to take a look at that autopsy report?"

"I'll run it past George, but he's going to say the same thing I'm going to say: wouldn't it make more sense for the family to pay for their own autopsy review?"

"Maybe. I'd prefer to get a completely objective outside analysis."

J.J. let out a long breath. "Okay. Whatever. But listen, West. I know this isn't what the family wants to hear, but I think there's a strong argument to be made that the professor offed herself."

Jason frowned. "Why do you say that?"

"To start with, she had a girlfriend, a boyfriend, and wasn't getting along with either of them."

"Okay. She had a complicated personal life."

"*You* have a complicated personal life. She was living out a soap opera."

"She taught film studies; maybe she thrived on drama."

"She was in debt."

Jason thought of next month's credit card bill. "Who isn't?"

"Seriously in debt. She'd maxed out all her cards—and she had a lot of cards."

"Financial strain. Fair enough."

"Her book deal fell through."

"She was writing a book?"

"Yep. She'd been working on it for years."

"Fiction? Nonfiction?"

"Nonfiction. Something about obscure or lost private detective films. Her agent pitched it to a couple of New York publishing houses, and one showed serious interest, but it turned out another editor had already acquired a similar book for that year's catalog. I don't know how it works, but her book wasn't going to be published."

"That would be disappointing, but wouldn't her agent just keep pitching the book?"

"I don't know. I guess? But according to police interviews with the boyfriend *and* the girlfriend, Ono was depressed about it."

"Okay, it's hearsay, but I agree this goes toward establishing our victim's state of mind."

"And, finally, she learned she wasn't getting tenure, which I guess is a very big deal for college professors."

"Yes, that would be a big deal." Jason thought it over, admitted, "It's a lot of bad news all at once."

"Yep. That's my thought."

"Well, we're after the truth, so—"

"*Are* we? My impression is we're after making a former senator feel better about his granddaughter's death. Which is, in my opinion, a waste of our time and resources."

Sure, it sounded callous, but J.J. had a point. Senator Ono was receiving consideration and treatment that most people, equally heartbroken but not rich and politically connected, wouldn't.

"If we're not working on this, we're working on something else, right?"

"That's right, and it could be something a hell of a lot more important."

"And you'll continue to work those cases," Jason pointed out. "You've still got your regular caseload. I'm the one being asked to prioritize this investigation, and, one way or the other, I've got to close it within thirty days."

J.J. muttered something that sounded astonishingly like, "But your cases are more fun." He seemed to be only half kidding.

Which reminded Jason.

"Hey," he said awkwardly, "Kapszukiewicz mentioned you phoned her on my behalf. I just wanted to say thanks."

"It probably did more harm than good," J.J. admitted with rare self-awareness. "But you're welcome. I mean, you're an asshole a lot of the time, but you're not the worst agent I've worked with."

Jason managed not to laugh. "You flatter me."

"Probably," J.J. agreed.

CHAPTER FOUR

They didn't build homes like Swanlea anymore.

Granted, they didn't build senators like Francis Ono anymore either.

But back to the house. The classically beautiful English country manor had been designed in 1919 for singing cowgirl Tally Valentine. Originally a hunting lodge, the rustic structure was transformed into a four-story, twenty-five-room mansion complete with stables, servants' quarters, tennis courts, and swimming pool. The singing cowgirl had lived among the classical ceiling frescos and gold-leaf-mirrored decorative niches until her death in 1979.

A year later the home had been purchased by then-senator Francis Ono, and the Ono family had lived there ever since.

From the start, Ono had been a controversial figure. A Dem who switched parties after his election, he'd been a big proponent of nuclear energy and a big opponent of the Equal Rights Amendment. Just to keep everyone confused, he'd been pro-Labor, pro-Education, and pro-Healthcare. He'd retired from the US Senate in 2012 but was still a force to be reckoned with in California politics. In fact, his surprise endorsement of Clark was a large part of why Jason's brother-in-law was now a junior representative for the Golden State.

Jason had never met Ono—he did not attend political functions, especially political functions held for Clark—and he assumed Ono did not know of him or connect him to the West family's political dynasty.

A surprisingly youthful housekeeper dressed in funereal-black led him to a sumptuous library where, despite the warmth of the day, the former legislator stood before a roaring fireplace beneath a life-sized portrait of himself, painted probably three decades earlier. He was drinking brandy.

The housekeeper stood silently in the doorway until Ono turned his head. Ono stared for a long moment at Jason.

"Special Agent West, I presume?"

"Senator Ono." Jason stepped forward to offer his credentials, but Ono waved him impatiently away. He pointed to a pale-blue brocade sofa.

"Sit. Brandy?"

Jason had only ever seen photos and footage of Ono, and he realized he was still expecting to encounter that very large and vigorous physical presence. Ono was now in his eighties. He was shrunken and frail. His sallow skin was mottled with age spots, though his brows, intimidating mustache, and toupee were all defiantly ink black. There was a tremor in the hand that jabbed at the sofa.

Jason politely declined the brandy and took a seat on the sofa where Ono indicated. Ono continued to stand over him, glaring down.

"We need to get something straight, Agent. Georgette did not kill herself."

"Right. The coroner's verdict was accidental death."

"*Possible suicide*," Ono spat out. "I read every word of that garbage report. If you'd known my granddaughter, you'd understand how ridiculous, how insulting to her memory the very idea of suicide is."

Jason did not take offense at Ono's tone or the finger wagged aggressively at his nose. He got it. Ono's response to grief was anger, and he was looking for someone or something on which to vent that anger. Jason just happened to be the nearest available target.

He kept his voice quiet and courteous. "Sir, I know this is difficult. I know you're not satisfied with the original investigation, which is why I'm here. I promise I'll look at everything—"

"That's not what I want! I want the Bureau to conduct its *own* investigation. From scratch. That's what I've asked for."

"Absolutely. That's my intent."

"I don't trust the police."

"I'm sorry to hear it."

"I don't trust anyone!"

"Okay, well..." Jason offered a smile. "I accept your challenge."

Ono glowered from beneath those black, bristling brows. "I don't want to be humored, Agent."

"Senator Ono, I'm sure you know the Bureau doesn't expend resources on humoring people."

Ono's upper lip curled. "*Now* you're being diplomatic."

"I try. May I ask why you reject the idea of accidental death?"

"Because it wasn't an accident."

"Right. How do you know that?"

"Because it's too great a coincidence. Georgette feared for her life. The idea that she would then die accidentally in such a stupid, ugly way strains belief!"

Coincidences did happen, of course, though law enforcement was naturally skeptical of them.

"Why did your granddaughter fear for her life?"

Ono's shoulders slumped. He shook his head.

Jason said, "She must have said something that made you think she was afraid. Did someone threaten her?"

"Possibly."

Wasn't that a yes or no question?

"Did your granddaughter have any enemies?"

Ono said impatiently, "*Everyone* has enemies."

Okay, well, maybe so. Jason probably had enemies—he certainly had a homicidal stalker. Sam had enemies.

"Did your granddaughter name names? Was there a specific person she thought might wish her harm?"

Ono hesitated. "Not that I recall."

Maybe he *was* trying to recall, or maybe he was hedging. Sometimes a hesitation was just a hesitation.

Jason changed tack. "Tell me about Georgette. What was she like?"

"Hardworking. Dedicated. Passionate about her work."

That was a glowing performance review but not exactly illuminating. Hopefully, Professor Ono's friends and colleagues would be able to offer a little more insight.

Ono turned away to pour himself another brandy. Over his shoulder, he said, "As hard as it is to believe, I'm convinced my granddaughter's murder had something to do with that film club she belonged to."

This was new information. Either Ono hadn't previously shared this theory—because it was an afterthought?—or the investigating detectives gave it no credence. The former was the more likely scenario. Ono had been stewing for six months.

"A film club? Something affiliated with the college?"

"No. A kind of…I'm not sure what you'd call it. A social club. A supper club for collectors of rare films."

Assuming Ono was referring to 35mm and not VHS rarities like a Disney Black Diamond edition of *Aladdin* (which at most might bring in something in the $300 range), rare films did go for a lot of money. And whenever a lot of money was involved, the likelihood of crime, including violent crime, increased exponentially. Still.

"And this is an actual school organization or a private get-together?"

"Private. Invitation only. My understanding is they met monthly for dinner and would then watch a film from a member's collection."

"Gotcha. Who else is in this social club? Other instructors? Students? Did Georgette mention any names?"

Again, Ono hesitated. "No."

It was always concerning when the complainant chose to withhold information, but they weren't through here. He would give Ono time to rethink and then circle back.

"Do you know where the movie nights are held? Do they rent an on-campus theater for their screenings?"

"I don't believe there's any connection to the college. I think they meet at someone's home. I don't know whose. They might move around." Ono sat down heavily across from Jason. He stared into his brandy glass. "I didn't pay attention. That's the truth. I should have listened to her. But."

Jason tilted his head, listening for what Ono wasn't saying. "But what?"

Ono said wearily, "It was always extremes with Georgette. Everything was wonderful or everything was terrible. There was no in-between. She never had an ordinary day. She could be…tiring."

"You didn't take her concerns seriously?"

Ono said again, "I didn't pay attention. The last time we spoke I was upset to learn she'd resumed her relationship with that bastard she worked with. *He* was a member of that group. I'm sure of it. In fact, I think he's the one who got her involved with those fanatics."

The *bastard* Georgette worked with would be Balthasar Bardolf, a fellow professor and archivist at the UCLA Film and Television Archive. Film archivists were the librarians of the film and television industry. Their number-one job was to scan or digitize original recordings into a digital medium in order to preserve them for future generations. UCLA's archive was the second largest in the country (only the Library of Congress was larger), which meant Bardolf's was a prestigious gig. It made sense he might be a member of the kind of cinephile clique Ono was talking about.

"How long have you known Bardolf?"

"I never met him." Ono threw back his brandy in one eyebrow-raising gulp. He glared at Jason. "I didn't need to meet him. I know everything I need to know about him."

As a wise man once said, *uh-huh.*

Ono must have read Jason's thoughts because he added, "He was a bad influence on her."

"How so?"

"He encouraged her worst tendencies."

What did *that* mean? Bardolf egged on her poor spending habits or introduced her to kinky sex?

"Meaning?"

Ono said testily, "I'm not going to do your job for you, Agent. Do your due diligence, and you'll soon understand my antipathy for that bastard."

"Do you have reason to believe Bardolf might have wanted to harm your granddaughter?"

Interestingly, when Ono was about to prevaricate, his gaze bored in on Jason's.

"They fought all the time. I believe he was physically abusive. *And* they were competing for tenure."

Jason studied Ono's lined face. "Did your granddaughter accuse Bardolf of physical abuse?" If so, it wasn't anywhere in the files Jason had skimmed.

"Not in so many words."

No. The relevant word was the word not spoken. *Nope.*

"Aside from Bardolf, did Georgette ever mention anyone you think might be connected to this film club?"

Ono gave a harsh laugh. "I'm sure you're already aware of Eli Humphrey. He's another one of these shady film-collector characters. Georgette reported him to the FBI for being involved in film piracy and bootlegging."

Actually, Georgette had reported Humphrey to LAPD's Art Theft Detail. Detective Gil Hickok, who'd headed up ATD for the last twenty years, had contacted the FBI. But both teams had agreed there was insufficient evidence to charge Humphrey with anything beyond being a fanatical movie collector, and in this town, that was practically a requirement for citizenship.

Jason said, "This film club doesn't sound like the most congenial get-together, but what do you think would drive another member to harm Georgette?"

Ono's dark eyes lit up. "The last time I spoke to Georgette, she told me she'd discovered the existence of a valuable old movie previously believed to be lost. I'm sure she feared someone in the club was after that film."

Jason began, "Did Georgette actually *say* she feared—"

"Yes! She said, and I quote: 'Any one of those guys would murder me to get their hands on that film.'"

Okay, maybe yes, maybe no. Georgette could have meant it literally, but it did sound a bit hyperbolic, like: *My wife will kill me if I forget to pick up milk.*

Granted, some wives did kill when their spouses forgot to pick up milk. People could be unpredictable.

"What was the film?"

"I don't know. She didn't share the title. She did say it was a crime film from the 1950s and that it was listed on the...the lost film list."

Ah yes. The famous Lost Film List.

Jason liked movies—who didn't?—and he'd been part of a few investigations involving film piracy. The making and selling of bootleg films continued to be a booming business: the movie and TV industry projected $51.6 billion in losses to online piracy that year. Despite living next door to Hollywood, the movie biz was not his area of expertise, but he knew from his own experience within the art world that if Georgette Ono really *had* located a print of a much-sought-after rare or lost film, someone might have been willing to kill her to get their hands on it. Fanatical collecting was not limited to any one art form. Hell, there were people willing to shoot each other over trading cards in a Target.

He said, "That's very helpful. Thank you, sir. Is there anyone else you feel I should take a particularly close look at?"

Ask and ye shall receive. Ono launched into a list of possible suspects and potential enemies that rivaled the Hollywood blacklists of the '40s and '50s. Soup to nuts, students to night watchman, in Ono's opinion, no one had played too small a role in his granddaughter's life to escape special scrutiny.

Or at least, no one in Georgette Ono's personal and professional life. Unsurprisingly, the senator did not consider anyone closer to home a suspect, and it probably went without saying that he wouldn't appreciate Jason doing so. But according to the Bureau's latest homicide statistics, the vast majority—a staggering fifty-eight percent—of murdered women and girls were killed by intimate partners or other family members.

Given that his prime directive seemed to be to appease the former senator, Jason listened attentively, took notes, and kept his mouth shut. But while he was not going to upset the old man unnecessarily, he was also not going to allow him to limit the scope of this investigation. Kapszukiewicz had said that "the family" had trouble accepting the accidental-death verdict, but as far as Jason could tell, the only family member calling for further investigation was Ono. He found that interesting.

When the interview concluded, the slim, silent housekeeper reappeared to see Jason to the front door. He left Senator

Ono drinking brandy and staring somberly at his portrait over the fireplace.

CHAPTER FIVE

Hugo Quintana, the burly security guard who admitted him into Touchstone's towering thirty-four-story, luxury, glass-and-steel apartment complex, *clearly* thought Jason was up to no good.

Even after a quick conference with the onsite manager, Hugo insisted on accompanying Jason to the thirty-first floor, watching in grim silence as Jason unlocked the apartment formerly occupied by Georgette Ono. It was a keyless entry. Jason typed in the pin, pushed the door open, nodded pleasantly, and shut the door in Quintana's face.

He turned the deadbolt—it seemed Ono had not placed all her faith in technology— which slid home with a satisfying *clunk*.

Hefty security hardware and the presence of hypervigilant security seemed to answer one question.

Fourteen hundred square feet, floor-to-ceiling windows, premium wood-style plank flooring, a gourmet kitchen with custom Italian cabinetry, and state-of-the-art appliances answered another.

Jason had no idea what film studies professors earned, but an apartment at Touchstone went for anything from $4,000 (a broom closet maybe?) to $30,000 a month. Outside the budget of most college professors, surely. Most FBI agents too. But Professor Ono's apartment had been leased by her family, and it was through arrangement with the family that Jason was to occupy Ono's rooms while he worked her case.

Ono's papers, books, and personal effects were supposed to be preserved and waiting for him, and fingers crossed that was true. Families had a way of "editing" the historical record of any information they deemed unflattering to themselves or their loved ones. Which just went to prove that for some people there really *was* a fate worse than death.

Anyway, it was a nice place—bigger than his little bungalow—with lots of light and inspirational views of the ocean and mountains. There was patio access from both bedrooms and the living room. Tall glass doors led out onto a long, expansive balcony that allowed in a cool ocean breeze too high and refined to carry any whiff of smog.

The walk-in closets in the silver-and-white master bedroom still held Ono's clothes—and hats. A whole row of fedoras and felt hats in different colors were posed on blank-faced mannequin heads on the top shelf of her closet.

Now there was a door you'd want to keep shut at night.

The built-in shelves still held her photos and knickknacks. Not many of either.

Whoever had cleaned up the crime scene—if crime it was—had done an impressive job. Other than the fact that the queen-size bed with its upholstered white-leather, geometric headboard was missing its mattress and bedding, there was no sign anyone had ever stepped inside that silver-and-white, pristine space-capsule of a room, let alone died there.

Jason had seen the police-cam footage, however, and there was no forgetting those images.

The shelves in Ono's office were crowded with books and a few more bibelots. There were framed detective film posters on the walls and a weighty replica (presumably a replica) of the Maltese falcon statue from the film with Bogart and Astor. A computer sat on the desk, but according to his notes, it was brand-new and Ono had not finished setting it up at the time of her death. LAPD had examined Ono's phone and laptop, but found nothing of interest and returned them to the family. Jason had a copy of the computer forensic analysis of Ono's electronics and had to agree with the conclusion that there wasn't anything useful to be found. No threatening emails. No sinister meet-me-at-midnight texts.

If, after a full and thorough investigation, LAPD had failed to find anything suspicious, how likely was it Jason was going to stumble over a convenient clue, especially when the FBI did not, typically, investigate homicides.

Or at least, the homicides the Bureau concerned itself with tended to be those that threatened society as a whole: serial killers, for example, or hate crimes, or murder on federal property, or the murder of an elected or appointed federal official, like a senator. The murder of a retired senator's granddaughter was stretching things, but that was the way of the world. Exceptions could always be made for the rich, the famous, the powerful, or the lucky-enough-to-know-someones.

Which didn't alter the fact that Jason didn't work a lot of homicides. Granted, he'd been involved in more homicide cases since he'd met Sam, but his ordinary workday didn't involve much whodunit. He was grateful for this case, grateful for the chance to redeem himself in his superiors' eyes, but he couldn't help wondering if he'd been handed this one in an effort to keep him out of further trouble.

Or, possibly, punishment for getting into trouble in the first place.

Long-lost detective films notwithstanding, there really wasn't a lot to support the claim that LAPD had rushed, let alone botched, the investigation into Georgette Ono's death.

Did Senator Ono's insistence on foul play in the death of his granddaughter stem from his own feelings of guilt for not paying closer attention to what had been going on with her? Jason wasn't sure. If the coroner's office had ruled suicide, he could have better understood Ono's insistence that the case be reopened, but the family had been thrown a bone with that accidental-death verdict.

Maybe Ono knew something nobody else did? More than once during their interview, Jason had the feeling the senator was withholding information. But he'd also suspected that, in his grief, Ono was grasping at straws.

The challenge was always to separate what had happened from what people *thought* had happened. Witness testimony was famously unreliable, and one of the main reasons for that had to do with the limitations of memory. Memories could fade, degrade, yes. But memory also had a way of evolving to accommodate new information. Georgette Ono had died six months earlier, so it was safe to assume both erosion and embellishment in the memories of all who'd known her. Certainly, half a year ago there had been no mention of legendary lost films or sinister cinephiles.

Jason didn't discount anything he'd learned from Senator Ono, but he had a whole hell of a lot of verifying to do, and not a lot of time in which to do it.

He was shaving his head in the spa-like master bathroom when Sam phoned.

Jason put down the razor and answered his cell. "Hey. What's up?" Sam didn't typically phone during the workday, but every so often their cases intersected.

"How was your flight?"

"Not bad." They had been in touch, of course, but had spoken less frequently while Jason had been out of the country. Even then, Sam had probably learned way more about Dutch museums than he'd ever wanted to know.

"And the meeting with de Haan's girlfriend?"

Honestly, Jason was surprised Sam even remembered he'd been meeting with Anna the day before. Then again, not many things slipped Sam's mind.

"Sad. She's brokenhearted. But I'm glad I went. She didn't know that Hans planned to ask her to marry him or that he'd made up his mind to take a leave of absence."

In fact, at first Jason wasn't sure it had been a good idea to tell Anna any of that. But after she'd stopped crying, she'd insisted she was glad to know de Haan's plans. She had struck him as a realist. She understood the choices de Haan had made, disastrous as they had proved.

"Good. Glad it was successful." Sam sounded preoccupied. Jason could hear the soft *click* of computer keys in the background. "How's the case?"

"Early days, but…interesting."

"Are you getting settled in?"

Not that Jason wasn't happy to hear from Sam, but this was kind of strange. Sam wasn't one for chitchat. Or at least not workday chitchat. He wondered uneasily if there was another reason for this call, something Sam wasn't looking forward to telling him.

"Yep. Staying in Ono's apartment is a useful setup. Is everything okay?"

Did Sam hesitate? His "Yes" was firm enough.

Jason steeled himself to ask. "Is there any update on Kyser?"

The soft clicking stopped. Jason heard the *squeak* of Sam's chair. "No. I'm sorry. Nothing so far."

"Nothing to be sorry for. It's not your fault."

"We're going to get him. It's just a matter of time."

Jason managed a brisk, "Yep. I know."

"In the meantime, you're off the grid. You've got some room to breathe."

"Right. Yes." Not for the first time, Jason wondered if the Ono case had deliberately been pitched to him as a softball. He considered. If the purpose of this call wasn't to bring him up to speed, then Sam wanted to talk for another reason.

Jason asked. "How are things there?"

Sam made a sound that wasn't quite a laugh. "Funny you should ask. There's a possibility Berkle wasn't acting alone."

Berkle... Why was that name so familiar?

"Says who?"

"Says his logbooks."

Logbooks? Oh, right. Oh *hell*. Berkle had been a long-haul trucker. Sam was talking about Oregon and the Roadside Ripper case.

Jason asked, "Who's the possible accomplice?"

"An unknown subject referred to only as Bone Road."

Jason asked, "Is that a CB handle or a pet name or what?"

"Your guess is as good as mine. So far, it's a dead end."

That was the problem with shooting your prime suspect. Not that Sam had shot him. That had been the work of a local deputy sheriff who had, in Sam's words, *formed an attachment* to Special Agent Adam Darling.

Awkward things, attachments.

Jason glanced down at the pile of hair lying in the bathroom sink like a soft black nest, glanced back at the man in the mirror. He couldn't decide if he looked more like a skinhead or a chemo patient. His face was all sharps and angles, his green eyes looked huge and feverish.

Either way, he did not look like himself. That was the goal.

He asked, "Does this mean the band's getting back together?"

"What's that?" Jason could hear the frown in Sam's voice.

"Are you putting the Roadside Ripper task force back together?"

"Ah. Not exactly. More like a symposium with some of our key players."

"Adam Darling?" Jason suggested.

"Correct."

"Travis Petty." That one wasn't a question. Jason had no doubt Petty would get himself on that task force—oh, sorry, *symposium*—whether Sam thought of it first or not. But Sam would, of course, think of Petty. Petty had been on the original taskforce, and Sam thought highly of his abilities.

And sure enough, Sam said neutrally, "Petty's an obvious choice."

"Mm-hm." The fact that it was true didn't make it any less irritating.

Sam spoke quietly to someone on the other end. He came back on the line. "Sorry. We're going to have to cut this short."

"Right. Thanks for touching base."

That was bound to sound like a weird comment. Because it *was* a weird comment.

Sam didn't seem to notice. "I'll try to phone tonight."

"Sure. It's fine if you can't, though, Sam. Everything's under control here."

"I never doubted it." Sam's tone was wry. "I still like hearing your voice last thing at night."

Okay. That was nice. That went a long way to soothing Jason's irritation at the thought of Sam once again working side by side with SA Petty. "Same," he said softly. "Talk to you later."

Ono's apartment felt very empty after Sam cut the connection.

Jason sighed, regarded his reflection.

It had been a decade since he'd worn an earring, but he'd had his ear repierced in Amsterdam. He pushed in the small diamond stud and regarded the result critically. Yeah, that worked.

The shaved head, the stylish stubble that wasn't quite a beard, the earring, and... Jason reached for a pair of fashion glasses with oversize black frames.

He slid the glasses on, tilted his head, considered himself. "I think so."

He did not look like an FBI agent. That was for sure. He looked like a trying-*way*-too-hard adjunct professor who was more than likely going to end up sleeping with one of his students.

He winked at his reflection.

Art, like the devil, was all in the details.

CHAPTER SIX

"So tell me, Special Agent West, what do you want from me that the files can't tell you?"

Detective Lacey Child was tall, dark-haired and, despite the fact that she looked to be in her late forties, very pregnant. Which probably accounted for the note of exasperation in her voice, and definitely accounted for the swollen feet propped on her desk.

In addition to its own Emergency Medical Services, UCLA had its own police force located on Westwood Avenue and serving a community of nearly eighty-three thousand faculty, staff, and students. A jurisdiction larger than most cities. The two-story station housed a 24/7 Dispatch Center, a Community Services Bureau, and Emergency Response teams.

All that said, UCPD had not handled the investigation into Georgette Ono's death. UCPD had worked with LAPD, but Ono had died in her Wilshire Blvd. apartment, and LAPD had led the investigation.

"The files paint a clear picture of Ono's death. I'm hoping for some insight into her life. Her work life, anyway."

Child said sardonically, "And you think her work life involved a lot of contact with the police?"

"A guy can hope." Jason was sort of kidding and sort of not. LAPD had done a very thorough job in building their case. "I'm not challenging the investigation, but I've got a grieving family trying to come to terms with a tragedy."

Child sighed. "Hey, I get it. The old man still has a lot of clout in Washington. I don't take offense."

"What a relief," Jason replied. "That was my biggest worry."

To give Child her due, she chuckled. "A G-man with a sense of humor. That's a new one. Granted, you don't look like a G-man."

"That's the idea."

"An idea which, for the record, seems a little over-the-top to those of us in this building, but the administration is one hundred percent behind your cloak-and-dagger op—I'm sure they're hoping the Ono family will donate a new wing in the professor's name—so ask me whatever you like."

"According to her grandfather, Professor Ono expressed fears for her safety shortly before her death. Did she report those concerns to UCPD?"

"Fears for her safety? No."

Jason considered that noncommittal reply. "Did she report other concerns?"

Child grimaced. "I may as well tell you I disagreed with the possible-suicide determination."

He was not entirely surprised at her frankness. Child struck him as a straight shooter. "I see."

"As a matter of fact, I wasn't convinced Ono's death was accidental, but it wasn't my—our—case. It *could* have been accidental. But suicide? I really struggle with that one, and I'm not surprised the family does too."

"Did you know Professor Ono?"

"Not well. Not personally. However, I had plenty of contact with her."

The fact that Child made that distinction furthered her credibility as far as Jason was concerned.

"As a victim or a..."

"Neither, really. She was, well, let's just say she was an *extremely* contentious personality."

"Meaning?"

Child made a sound that fell somewhere between a laugh and a groan. "There was no infraction of rules too small for her to overlook, or report. Parking violations. Smoking on campus. Copyright violations. That last one was a big one for her."

"You're kidding."

"No. You'd have thought she had some kind of spyware on the library copiers, the number of times she was in here reporting the unauthorized reproduction of magazine and newspaper articles."

"Hm. That's different."

"I've never seen anything like it in twenty years of policing. That woman argued with people online, offline..."

"And all around the town?"

"Pretty much. Yeah."

"Who was she arguing with online?"

"She was active on gaming sites. There's a game called *L.A. Noire.* She was all into that, and there's nothing wrong with gamers and gaming, but she argued *constantly* with people on the community portal. Oh, and movie sites. She fought with people on the TCM forum, for God's sake. They were threatening her life on Reddit."

Jason opened his mouth, but before he could ask the obvious question, Child said, "Absolutely. We looked into every possible line of inquiry. No one came out of the internet to get her."

"What about her real-life confrontations?"

"She had a messy personal life, no question. Campus security was called on one occasion to break up an argument between her and Calida Lois—that was the girlfriend. She's some kind of indie film director. I believe at one time they were going to make a movie together. I can only imagine. After that fell through, they continued a personal relationship. Apparently there was a physical altercation on Friday night— the same night we theorize Ono died."

"Right."

"There was also an on-again-off-again boyfriend. Balthasar Bardolf. He's an instructor here on campus."

Jason nodded. "Bardolf is Ono's grandfather's prime suspect."

"I know. He has an alibi."

"I thought there was some question as to the exact time of death?"

"Correct. But Bardolf was out of town the entire three-day weekend. That said, yes, in a homicide investigation, he'd certainly have warranted a closer look."

"I see." He still warranted a closer look, in Jason's opinion.

"For one thing, he owed her quite a bit of money."

"Do we know for what?"

"This, that, and the other. Which is probably why she was having difficulty collecting. Speaking of which, Ono had a sizable film collection Bardolf tried to lay partial claim to."

"I don't recall seeing that noted anywhere."

"It didn't go anywhere. He had zero documentation, zero evidence to prove his claim."

Jason said, "Given the senator's antipathy toward him, Bardolf would've been in for a fight even with proof of purchase."

Child's expression spoke volumes, but she restrained herself to a mild, "Agreed."

"What happened to Ono's film collection?"

"The family donated it to the archive."

"UCLA's film archive?"

She intoned, *"At UCLA, there can be only one."*

Jason grinned at the *Highlander* riff. "So in a way, Bardolf may get his hands on Ono's collection after all?"

Child shook her head. "It's all about ownership for these fanatics. That's what collecting is. Possession. Ownership." She frowned. "What's so funny?"

"Nothing. You're one hundred percent correct about that. It's just funny hearing it from someone who isn't ACT. I mean, maybe it's generational. NFTs are changing the art world and collecting."

"I don't pretend to get the whole NFT thing."

"Supposedly, the virtual goods market will reach nearly $190 billion by 2025. But yeah, for most art collectors it's still about to have and to hold."

"I think it's all a scam." Child sighed. "Anyway, I don't want to give you the wrong impression. To meet Ono, to chat with her, she was pleasant. I'm sure my failure to imprison Dr. Fisk for copying cartoons from *The New Yorker* was a big disappointment, but I never had any problems with her. She used to always bring in a box of Japanese delicacies for us at New Year's."

"That was nice of her."

"It was. She was thoughtful and considerate. She wasn't driven by malice. But that…rigidity made her very unpopular. If you were late to class, you'd find the doors locked. If she caught you checking your cell phone, you were out. No iffs, ands, or buts. No second chances. I mean, she was teaching film studies, which I'd think was a pretty easy course, but she was one of the most disliked instructors on campus. What does that tell you?"

"Hard to say. Given everything you've laid out, why do you think the possibility of homicide was dismissed?"

Child made a sound of disgust. "I could speculate."

"Hey. Please do."

"My colleagues at LAPD believed the strongest argument was for suicide. She'd been having difficulties with the administration, which seemed to peak after a group of ultraconservative students threatened the university with legal action over a course Ono taught called the Celluloid Closet. The administration isn't talking. They acknowledge that she was denied tenure but insist it had nothing to do with the lawsuit. Tenure was granted to Bardolf, incidentally, which, I guess, could've factored into her depression."

"That's a hit to the ego, but is it reason to kill herself?"

"She was very much in debt thanks to that expensive film-collecting habit."

"Financial stressors can definitely play a role in suicide. But I've seen her apartment, which the family—her grandfather—paid for, by the way, so it's hard to imagine a cash flow problem so severe it would drive her to suicide."

Jason surmised someone with Ono's background would have a trust fund. Granted, like Jason, Ono might have been determined to not draw from her trust until she was retirement age. Or she might have already run through her trust buying up rare movies.

"And then there was the book deal that went south."

"That would be disappointing," Jason agreed. "But isn't that how it works? Don't authors always have a million rejections before they get published?"

"Don't ask me. I do know that publishing is a big-ass deal on this campus. It's tied to getting tenure."

"Okay. Well."

"At the time of her death she had broken up with both Lois and Bardolf."

"Relationship problems are a big one. Fair enough." Having come so close to losing Sam, Jason could relate. He'd felt sick, even desperate on that long flight back from Montana when he had been so sure it was over between them. He hadn't been suicidal, but it was the only time he could remember being completely indifferent to extreme turbulence on an aircraft.

Would juggling two romantic partners halve your emotional investment in each person? Double your overall emotional investment? Hard to say. He found the idea of polyamory stressful in itself. Or maybe that was because the idea of two Sam Kennedys was enough to short-circuit anyone.

Child said sardonically, "If you want my honest opinion, I think Ono was dismissed as a sexually confused, possibly troubled woman involved in a messy romantic triangle and into kinky sex and, worse, 'art films.'"

Jason laughed, though it wasn't funny. He'd gotten that same feeling reading over Ono's case files. Which, given that police reports weren't supposed to be colored by things like feelings or emotions, was kind of telling.

"So the consensus was she committed suicide." It wasn't a question because it seemed clear Child had been the lone voice in the wilderness.

"Yep. As far as the method of strangulation, the forensic evidence was inconclusive. She certainly could have placed the rope around her neck and tied it to the closet rod. And the rod was high enough that even if she didn't actually lose consciousness, she might have been so oxygen deprived she couldn't regain her footing in time."

"She used a slipknot," Jason pointed out.

"She still would've had to pull the rope to free herself. If she blacked out or was too foggy to think clearly..." Child shrugged.

Jason remembered those not-crime-scene-slash-crime-scene photos. "The bruises on her body could have come from the altercation with Lois earlier that evening."

"Exactly."

Jason considered. "Not my area of expertise, but it seems like trying to masturbate in the midst of committing suicide would be...distracting."

Sam would probably know the answer to that one. Sam knew the answer to a lot of things that made most people uncomfortable.

Child bobbed her head side to side in a *maybe-yes-maybe-no*. "Psychologically, that's a legit question. Which is where they found the wiggle room to rule accidental death. That, and the fact that she was found surrounded by porn and sex toys."

Right. The porn and sex toys—and the lack of a suicide note—were a strong argument in favor of accidental death. Ono having had a lot of stressors in her life just emphasized why she might have been more distracted, less careful than usual, during her playtime.

Child seemed to read his mind. "The issue I have with accidental death is, she was a control freak. She wasn't a woman to make mistakes."

"Yeah, but if it wasn't suicide and it wasn't an accident, then Professor Ono did make a mistake. She made the mistake of trusting the wrong person—and it proved fatal."

* * * * *

It had been a busy afternoon on top of the eleven-hour flight from Amsterdam to Los Angeles. Also, Amsterdam was nine hours ahead, so by the time Jason pushed out through the glass doors of UCPD's brick building, he was feeling every mile and minute of his jet lag.

Which was probably why he didn't notice the slim man with curly blond hair and blue eyes until they were just about face-to-face.

The man gave Jason a polite smile and nod. Jason gave an absent smile in return—and just managed not to do a double take.

The man's expression changed. He looked momentarily confused.

They passed each other, and Jason kept walking.

He'd known there was a possibility he might run across Alexander Dash—hell, there was a chance he might run into one of his old professors or even a former classmate now working on a doctorate—but he'd figured there would be time to sidestep any actual encounter.

Alexander—Alex—taught art at UCLA. He was a friend of Charlotte's, and after the first time Sam had dumped Jason, Charlotte had tried to set Jason up with Alex. And, in fact, Jason found Alex attractive and interesting. He just found Sam *more* attractive and interesting. Than anyone. Than everyone.

Anyway, even if Alex thought Jason looked familiar, UCLA was a huge campus, and there was a very good chance they wouldn't run into each other again.

If they did, it wasn't the end of the world. Alex knew Jason worked for the FBI, but it wasn't as though he was involved in Jason's case.

Briefly, Jason wondered what had brought Alex to the police station. He hadn't looked particularly worried or anxious, so hopefully nothing more serious than something to do with parking tags or checking the lost and found.

CHAPTER SEVEN

If Hugo Quintana had been suspicious of Jason before, it was nothing to his level of distrust after he realized Jason had altered his appearance.

Nor did he accept Jason's off-hand, "I didn't realize there was a dress code," as an explanation. Quintana was equally unconvinced by the exasperated property manager's assurance that Jason had permission to stay in Professor's Ono apartment. Once again he insisted on accompanying Jason to the thirty-first floor.

It was tempting to whip out the old tin and dazzle Quintana with police science, but Jason understood the reason behind the hypervigilance, even if it was belated.

When they at last reached Ono's apartment, Jason unlocked the door using the pin code. As the electronic lock turned over, Quintana growled, "I have my eye on you."

"That's very flattering, but I'm engaged." Jason closed the door in Quintana's face. Just before the door settled into the frame, Jason saw Quintana's complexion turn puce, saw the fury in his black eyes.

We are not amused.

Might be a good idea to have Russell take a look at Touchstone's security team. Presumably LAPD had run a basic background check on anyone who might conceivably have access to Ono's apartment, but LAPD had been operating on the assumption that Ono killed herself.

And security personnel? Well, results may vary.

He walked down the short hall to the atomic blast of light that was the living room. He was starving. The cheese and pickle sandwich of that morning felt like another lifetime. There hadn't been time to pick up anything in the way of groceries, so hopefully Quintana and Co. would lower the drawbridge for a DoorDasher.

Jason heeled out of his shoes, shrugged off his jacket, pulled off his shoulder rig, and flung himself on the long and not particularly comfortable white couch.

He'd catnap for ten minutes, then he'd rustle up some dinner, then he'd take another, closer look at the case files, noting his thoughts and observations, and *then* he'd prepare for class tomorrow.

It sounded exhausting...

When he opened his eyes, it was dark and the entire room was shaking.

Earthquake.

Jason sat up, groggy and disconnected, realizing he was lying on a...padded table? In an unfamiliar room. For a second or two he thought he was back in Amsterdam, but no hotel in Amsterdam—in all of the Netherlands—had been this uncomfortable or noisy.

Ceiling fixtures were not falling, the cupboards were not emptying their contents onto the floor. Not an earthquake. That rumble was not the building coming apart, it was an engine. A plane was passing overhead.

He went to the glass doors and gazed out. He could see the anti-collision lights flashing red and white on the fuselage, wing, and tail tips. They looked close enough to touch, and a frisson of alarm rippled down his spine.

That thing had just missed— Had that thing just missed—

Holy hell.

He watched the plane grow smaller and smaller and finally disappear into a web of thready clouds.

Feeling for his phone, he saw it was nearly eight. That felt like a bigger disaster than nearly getting wiped out by a 747. He took another look around, trying to locate a lamp. Table lamps did not appear to be a thing Professor Ono was into.

He finally located the switch for the overhead lights in the hall.

Hard white light illuminated the ultramodern living room and kitchen. The place reminded him of a stage set, though it was hard to know how it had looked when Ono lived and worked there. Presumably she'd occasionally left a book lying on a table or a coffee cup sitting in the sink.

In Jason's opinion, you could tell quite a bit about people from their taste in art, but the artwork in Ono's living and dining rooms and kitchen was that kind of prefurnished stuff: silk plants, metal wall art, throw pillows that came with the furniture. No paintings or art photography. Granted, the lack of choice revealed character too.

The framed posters and movie memorabilia in Ono's office, the personal photos in the bedroom, made him think those were the rooms where she'd actually lived. The front rooms were for display. The modern equivalent of a Victorian era parlor.

He placed a food delivery order for grilled chicken Mexican Caesar salad, placed another order with Instacart for some basic groceries, then phoned down to notify the security desk that company was a-coming. He had just hung up when his cell phone rang and Sam's photo—Sam looking fractionally less forbidding than usual because the pic had been snapped during their brief vacation in Wyoming—popped up.

"Hi!" Jason was surprised. This was early for Sam to phone.

"Hey." Sam's voice sounded…off. Not soft exactly, but less terse than usual. "I hear you had a close call."

"I did? Did I? *Oh*, the plane."

"Jonnie heard it on the news. A 747 departing LAX nearly clipped the top of the Touchstone building."

Jason leaned back against the kitchen counter. He wasn't sure if that funny feeling in his chest was from realizing he'd genuinely had a close call or the fact that Sam was reaching out to him after the close call.

"I kind of missed it. I was napping."

"*Napping?*"

Jason laughed at Sam's tone. "Mere mortals occasionally need some shut-eye."

"You're jetlagged."

Something that Sam rarely seemed to experience. Maybe because he never seemed to sleep much regardless of time zones.

"Probably."

Neither said anything for a moment.

"How's the case?" Sam asked.

"The case? It's looking more and more like murder by death."

"I don't follow."

"I don't either really. The verdict seems to have been decided by committee."

"How so?"

"LAPD wanted to write the victim off as a suicide. UCLA's PD couldn't sign off on that. The ME couldn't determine either way because the victim wasn't found for four days and had been in a physical altercation on the evening death likely occurred. So, in consideration of the family—meaning a former senator—the case was closed as accidental death possible suicide."

Sam made a noncommittal *hm*.

"The family is struggling with the accidental-death verdict, let alone possible suicide. Her grandfather insists she was murdered. She does seem to have had a problematic personality."

"Would you like me to—"

"No, no," Jason said quickly. "I'm just thinking out loud. I was viewing this more as a diplomatic mission, but there might actually be a case worth investigating. How's it going there?"

"The usual bureaucratic bullshit."

"Right. I meant with the Roadside Ripper case. The possibility that Berkle might have had an accomplice."

It wasn't like Jason hadn't realized the personal implications for Sam in the news that Berkle might have had an accomplice. Obviously, Sam would have feelings about the possibility Berkle hadn't acted alone. Given Sam's belief that Ethan, his college boyfriend, had fallen prey to the Roadside Ripper, he had to be experiencing a painful mix of emotions.

But Sam said crisply, "As of now, that's all it is. A possibility. A theory."

And there was the catch-22. Emotionalism—his own or anyone else's—made Sam uncomfortable. Which in turn inhibited Jason's natural, quick sympathy. He knew Sam sometimes found his reactions a little "operatic." The trick was finding the balance between supportive and, er, startling.

When Sam had phoned earlier that afternoon, he'd seemed to think the theory of Berkle's accomplice was credible, and his instinct had been to talk to Jason. To turn to Jason. But that impulse had passed.

"Right. Well."

At the same time, Sam said, "I just wanted to touch base. Make sure you were..."

Alive? He'd have known if Jason wasn't. If that plane had hit Touchstone, it would have been all over the news. This was probably another instance of WWWD. Sam doing what he figured Jason would do, what Jason would expect. Which didn't make it any less heartfelt on Sam's end—or gratifying on Jason's.

He missed Sam. He would have given a lot just to spend tonight together at home—either of their homes, or hell, even a hotel room—just sharing a meal and talking.

Jason smiled. "Thanks. It's always nice hearing your voice."

Sam said sardonically, "I know. I get that a lot."

And people said Kennedy had no sense of humor.

Jason chuckled, and Sam said in that softer voice he typically reserved for late night calls, "Have a good night, West. I'll talk to you tomorrow."

Jason spent the rest of the evening going through Professor Ono's desk and papers.

He found a printed manuscript titled *Hollywood Detour* and the accompanying rejection letter.

He glanced through the pages, read a little of the introduction.

Lost films have a resonance beyond film history. They can help correct the historical record. They offer scholars an opportunity to see historical figures like Sir Arthur Conan Doyle or Teddy Roosevelt in action. They frequently feature real settings, forever preserving fragments of the past in amber: a detail of fashion, a type of automobile, a shot of a long-gone street. They help the contemporary viewer better understand how those who came before us lived, laughed, loved—and, in the case of crime films, died.

Granted, you could say that about all art, but film had the advantage of showing people in motion, and people in motion were awkward and vulnerable and human in a way people in a portrait were not.

He wondered what had attracted Ono to detective films specifically. It seemed a safe deduction given the Maltese falcon statue, the closet full of fedoras, and the movies posters of *Chinatown*, *The Big Sleep*, and *The Long Goodbye*.

Maybe it was in keeping with her *inner control freak*, as Detective Child had put it. Mystery movies explored the dark side of the human psyche, but detective films did more. They not only tried to explain the often inexplicable; they tried to bring resolution, even deliver justice.

What mysteries had Ono struggled to make sense of? What injustices had she wished to see remedied?

From the rejection letter, it was clear Ono's agent had still been one hundred percent behind the project, still been confident they would place the manuscript at a publishing house, although it was looking more and more like it would be a smaller university press.

Since the objective for a professor seeking tenure would be publication with any reputable publishing house, it seemed to Jason that this motive for suicide could safely be scratched.

By then it was pretty late, and he turned to Professor Dahle's notes and lesson plans. Dahle, a first-year assistant professor, was enjoying a few weeks of paid sick leave while Jason "covered" his classes. Jason's plan had simply been to show movies and lecture rooms full of the most likely suspects on the fallacy of piracy as a victimless crime, but it seemed Dahle had higher ambitions for them both. After spending an hour trying to decipher pages and pages of Dahle's microscopic scratchings, he turned to Ono's bookshelves for both relief and inspiration.

Ono had about thirty books on film studies. More books on film theory, acting, directing, and several books on film preservation. And entire shelf was devoted to film noir.

He selected *Queer Images: A History of Gay and Lesbian Film in America* as his bedtime reading, and headed for the guest room.

Like the rest of the apartment, the decor was stylishly nondescript. Gray and white walls, gray and white bedding, silver-framed mirrors, and white built-ins. A dead African violet sat on one mirrored quatrefoil nightstand. A clock that had missed a time change or two sat on the other.

It was unexpectedly quiet up here with the clouds and stars—and despite the occasional plane. The Touchstone architects had invested in some serious noise reduction.

Jason undressed, washed up, and walked to the floor-to-ceiling glass doors, gazing out at the panoramic view of the tops of other sky-rises and busy city streets. Professor Ono had literally lived in an ivory tower. Okay, well, the tower wasn't literally ivory, but the architectural attitude was.

Ono had spent her days trying to teach kids who didn't like her about the value of a rapidly changing medium that recorded a world no longer in existence. And at night she sat up here, gazing down at buildings and streets filled with people going about their lives—from a perspective so removed, she might as well have been watching ants chasing breadcrumbs.

Or a movie from a distance?

What did you want?

What did anyone want?

Funny to think he'd been a flick of an airplane's wing from death this evening, and he'd never seen it coming. Maybe *funny* wasn't the word. The problem with death was it never happened at a convenient time. There was always, always going to be too much left unfinished, unsaid.

Aside from everything else, what a weird way that would have been for things to end between himself and Sam.

But they weren't unique in that. That's how it was for everyone. How it had been for Ono and her many complicated relationships, surely? Was it possible she had ended both relationships deliberately, knowing she was going to take her life? Were the arguments an attempt to give closure to Bardolf and Lois? Or to punish them?

Or just an awful coincidence that Ono happened to die while on the outs with two people who should have been closest to her?

He shook off the morbid thought. But he was in a morbid business, and a new and grimmer thought took its place.

Maybe there was no accomplice. Maybe Berkle *had* acted alone. Double acts made up slightly less than a quarter of all serial killings. Maybe Ethan could stay safely buried—if not forgotten—in Sam's psyche.

One wrong move. That's all it took.

Maybe Professor Ono had everything she wanted.

Maybe she had not given up or climbed, metaphorically speaking, onto a cracked rung. Maybe she had simply miscalculated, lost her footing.

And so...lights out.

Jason sighed, turned from the window, and climbed into the double bed. There was no art in this room either, but a black-framed poster of a poem by D.H. Lawrence hung across from the bed.

WHEN I WENT TO THE FILM

*When I went to the film and saw all the black-
and-white feelings that nobody felt,*

*And heard the audience sighing and sobbing
with all the emotions they none of them felt,*

*And saw them cuddling with rising passions
they none of them for a moment felt,*

*And caught them moaning from close-up
kisses, black-and-white kisses that could not
be felt,*

*It was like being in heaven, which I am sure
has a white atmosphere*

*Upon which shadows of people, pure
personalities*

Are cast in black and white, and move

In flat ecstasy, supremely unfelt

And heavenly.

CHAPTER EIGHT

"Following the Supreme Court's ruling that movies didn't have First Amendment protection, local governments passed laws restricting the public exhibition of 'indecent' or 'immoral' films."

The trio of jocks half lounging on the top riser settled more comfortably and prepared for sleep. Jason mentally sighed and kept talking.

"Public pressure resulted in the establishment of a national censorship board, which in 1930 became the Motion Picture Production Code. You may have heard it referred to as the Hays Code."

"But why wouldn't movies have First Amendment protection?" someone called out from the second row.

"Good question. Because the court believed film and the film industry could too easily be manipulated and used for *eville*."

This earned several titters and a couple of outright laughs.

"The major principle governing the code was that no picture would be produced which could lower the moral standards of viewers. This wasn't just about avoiding the prurient or the gratuitous, though that certainly was part of it. The idea was, the sympathy of the audience should never be with criminals. Not just with criminals, though. In this context, *evildoers* included anyone who flouted societal norms and conventions. For example, a woman who left her husband and child to be with her lover shouldn't be surprised to find herself beneath the wheels of a train before the end credits."

Eye rolls, mutters, some laughs, and a lot of glances at the clock on the wall. The jocks in the back slumbered peacefully on. If Jason had actually been teaching this course, he'd have to, eventually, do something about that back row, but happily, not his problem. Frankly, he'd rather tackle a dozen gun-toting art smugglers than a row of smart-ass college kids. At least in the former case he could arrest the assholes.

"By the way, there're plenty of people and organizations on both sides of the political spectrum that still feel films and filmmakers should adhere to a particular vision of morality or ethics or political correctness, whatever you want to call it. But anyway, in 1968 the Production Code was replaced by the MPAA film rating system, which is still in effect. Sort of."

But I digress.

He was liable to digress a lot given that these were topics he tended to be passionate about. He and Sam frequently debated the positive and negative aspects of censorship. Sam took a ruthlessly pragmatic view. He was always going to view artistic integrity as secondary to keeping people safe. Jason couldn't view artistic freedom as a black-and-white issue.

"Anyway, back when the production code was still in effect—and regardless of how sensitively they might be handled—certain behaviors would not appear in films. Nudity, for example. Profanity, drugs, white slavery, scenes of childbirth, and ridicule of the clergy were not permitted."

Unsurprisingly, these kids found the list more sidesplitting than shocking.

"By that token, films portraying homosexuality—listed under sexual perversion in the Code—in a positive or sympathetic light were no-go. Even the inference of homosexuality was no-go. As were films openly depicting interracial relationships, premarital or illicit sex, bearing children out of wedlock, and so forth. Which isn't to say that such films weren't made. Filmmakers had to get creative to figure out ways to make the movies they wanted to make. Which is what brings us here today."

And so on and so forth. Jason spent forty minutes relaying everything he'd crammed into his jetlagged brain the night before.

The good news was he'd remembered more than he'd thought he would. The bad news was, unless he could find someone to translate Professor Dahle's notes, he was going to end up doing as much or more homework for this class than these damned kids.

It wasn't like anyone in here was a suspect. The students who had attended Ono's classes six months ago were scattered to the four winds, i.e., enrolled in other courses. By all accounts, Ono hadn't fraternized with her students. It was extremely unlikely she'd have allowed one into her apartment, especially at night. If anyone *had* been with her, it was someone she'd invited in. Someone she trusted.

No, Jason's so-called teaching was simply to provide cover for his snooping around campus, asking awkward questions and making a general nuisance of himself. With the exception of Senator Ono, no one was expecting much to come of this investigation. Jason? Jason needed a win, but he wasn't going to manufacture a case that didn't exist.

He couldn't help hoping that there *was* a case, though.

When the seminar concluded and the last student filed out, Jason popped a throat lozenge and tried once again to phone Calida Lois, Ono's indie director girlfriend. The woman she'd apparently had a physical confrontation with only hours before her death.

This was his fourth try. He'd phoned yesterday afternoon and left a message with the usual spiel about who he was and what he wanted, but had received no return call. He'd tried first thing that morning and again between classes, but no reply. So he wasn't hopeful he was going to catch the elusive Ms. Lois without hunting her down in person.

But on the second ring, she picked up with a flat, "Speaking."

"Ms. Lois? This is Special Agent West. I phoned earlier."

"Yes, I know. This is starting to feel like harassment." The intonation was African-American. Her voice was high and indignant.

"I apologize for giving that impression. Professor Ono's family is unsatisfied with the outcome of the initial investigation into her death, and I've been authorized to—"

"I know! *I know!*" Lois broke in. "They think *I* murdered Georgie, even though I'm the *only* person in her goddamned life who ever actually *cared* about her."

Jason had been prepared for defensiveness. Her fury gave him pause. He said—still neutral, still courteous, "No one has suggested anything remotely like that."

"Then you must not be listening because the old man *absolutely* believes it."

"I can only assure you that's not the theory he shared with me yesterday."

She didn't speak, but he could hear the angry rise and fall of her breathing.

"Ms. Lois—Calida—can we meet? I just want to talk to you. You knew Professor Ono better than anyone. I'd prefer to have this conversation in person."

She shrieked, "*Hell no, we can't meet!* Are you serious? You're not dragging me down to some police station or FBI office. I know how that goes. And I'm *not*—I repeat, *not*—giving you permission to enter my work space or my home or my—"

Jason held his cell away from his ear until the volume dropped to non-eardrum-piercing decibels. He said quickly, "What if we met for dinner? You choose where and when. I promise this isn't any kind of trap. I just want your insight."

Another one of those raspy pauses. There was a lot of pent-up—and not so pent-up—emotion there. Also a fair bit of paranoia. What the hell had the cops said to her during their investigation to make her feel so threatened?

He was sure she was going to turn him down flat, but once again she surprised him.

"Intercrew in KTown. Eight o'clock. Do *not* be late. And you'd *better* be alone." She hung up.

Oh. Kay. Well. That sounded both hopeful and ominous.

Jason pocketed his cell. He figured he had just enough time to make it to the phone-booth-sized office he'd been assigned in the basement—er, on the ground floor of the Archive Research and Study Center—in order to check his messages, grab his notes, and meet with Aric Bern, Chair of the Department of Film, Television, and Digital Media.

The UCLA campus had changed a lot since his student days, but he still knew a couple of shortcuts. The carillon bells were chiming as he strode through the arches of Royce Hall. Powell Library in sight, he nearly walked into a slender guy with tousled blond hair and—oh shit.

Alexander Dash.

Second time in two days? What were the odds of that? Apparently one hundred percent.

Alex, peering at his cell phone, barely glanced up at the near collision, but then did a double take.

"*Jason?*"

Jason considered and dismissed the idea of pretending he didn't recognize Alex. He summoned a quick smile. "Hey! Alex."

After yesterday, he'd known this was liable to happen, so why hadn't he headed if off by contacting Alex first?

Alex's smile held a tinge of bewilderment, his blue gaze flicking from Jason's shaved head to his black ankle-zipper boots. "It *is* you! I almost didn't recognize you."

Almost was not good enough. Maybe he should have gone ahead and dyed his hair and beard red.

Jason said with a cheeriness he didn't feel, "It's me!"

"What are you— Are you teaching here?"

"I am, yeah."

"You're not with the FBI?"

Jason swore inwardly and kept smiling for all he was worth. "Long story. Actually, did you want to grab a coffee and catch up?"

"Uh, sure. When?"

Jason did some quick recalculating. The meeting with Bern, though important, could be postponed. He definitely did not want Alex wandering around, perhaps speculating publicly about whether Jason still worked for the FBI.

"Now?"

Alex shook his head. "Sorry. I'm late for class now."

Jason swallowed his exasperation. "Right. How about lunch?"

Another regretful shake of Alex's head. "I've got an optometrist appointment. How about dinner?"

"I've got plans for dinner, but I'd love to grab a quick drink first."

Alex brightened. "That'd be great. How about the Tuck Room Tavern on Wilshire at six?"

Jason was already in motion, walking backward, saying, "Terrific. I'll see you then!"

Alex smiled, gave him a thumbs-up, and called—within earshot of at least fifty people, "Don't worry! Your secret's safe with me!"

"You!"

Once upon a time Jason had been reasonably popular with security personnel. But either his aftershave had turned or he'd lost his mojo because when he finally stepped out of the elevators into the dim, climate-controlled recesses of the

Archive Research and Study Center (ARSC), he was immediately accosted by a small, spry man in a navy-blue uniform. The guard had sparse yellow hair and glasses with lenses thick enough to adorn a cartoon character.

"Me?" Jason glanced around the deserted corridor, fully expecting to see some other miscreant. But nope. It appeared he was indeed the offender.

Up close, the little man was older, closer to retirement age than Jason had thought, and more irate.

"Students aren't allowed down here."

Jason tried to get a look at the name on the ID badge. The light was abysmal in this underground chamber, but he thought the last name was *MacIntyre.* "Sure. I'm not a student. I'm—"

"Unauthorized personnel are not allowed down here."

"Right. Mr. MacIntyre, is it? I'm—"

Like Hugo Quintana before him, this guy wasn't having anything Jason was selling.

"You'll have to leave now."

"I have identification."

"Pop!" Aric Bern stood in his office doorway. "This is Professor West. We're squeezing him in with us for the time being."

"*He's* a professor?" Pop protested.

"I'll try not to take that personally," Jason said.

Bern, tall, handsome, and silver-haired as an aging matinee idol, said patiently, "Remember? Professor West is covering for Professor Dahle while he's on sick leave?" He smiled. "Jason, meet Martin MacIntyre. Pop's an institution around these parts. He makes sure the doors stay locked and the vending machine stocked."

Pop was unswayed by flattery. "But what's he down *here* for? Instructors don't keep office hours down here."

Actually, nobody but Bern and a collections intern, two film prep technicians, and a handful of other archive-related staff kept office hours down there, which made it ideal for Jason's base camp.

Bern said apologetically, "That's true, but we're extremely short on office space on this campus."

Ono's office had been down here, but it was hard to say if that had been her isolating herself from all irritating others or her being isolated from irritated others.

"No problem," Jason assured him, as if all this hadn't already been settled. He offered his hand. "Nice to meet you, Pop."

Pop muttered something that was probably not *the pleasure's all mine*, and walked away.

Bern shook his head. "Anyway, it's good to see you again, Jason." He ushered Jason into a cozy office lined with shelves overflowing with books, DVDs, and movie memorabilia. A movie-screen-style frame of Bern with his wife and kids sat on his desk. A red, white, and black poster for Martin Scorsese's *Mean Streets* hung on the wall behind Bern's desk.

Bern closed the office door and beckoned Jason to a black canvas director's chair. "Don't mind Pop. He's getting cranky in his old age. But he's worth his weight in gold."

Which was probably how they'd originally paid him, given that he looked like he'd arrived with the building in 1927.

"Better to care too much than too little," Jason replied.

"He definitely cares, which is a good thing, given that our security budget isn't what it used to be."

Probably not. In 2015, the 450,000 films, TV shows, and other moving image materials, some dating all the way back to 1889, that made up UCLA's Film and Television Archive, had been moved to the monumental, state-of-the-art Stoa building in Santa Clarita, along with a good portion of the archive's staff. The university's Archive Research and Study Center continued to coordinate access to the archive through the Powell Library Media Lab, but the demand for security was hardly what it had been when the actual archive had been there to protect and preserve.

"I bet," Jason said. "We're all safety-minded these days."

"Yes, we are. Anyway. Did you run into any problems this morning? Is there anything I can do to facilitate your investigation?"

Jason had previously worked with Bern on two separate piracy investigations. He was unfailingly charming and helpful, but distracted. A very busy guy. Judging by the way Bern was trying not to look at the miniature silver and black Hollywood movie clapboard clock on his desk, it seemed not much had changed.

"What can you tell me about Professor Ono?"

Bern's brows rose. "I can tell you I was surprised when the administration informed me her case had been reopened."

"You had no trouble believing that her death was accidental or even possibly suicide?"

"I don't think she killed herself." Bern sounded definite. "Even accidental is a stretch. She was so cautious. So careful. She wasn't the kind of person who had accidents." He made a face. "Granted, I didn't know her as well as I imagined." He shook his head. "*That* was crazy."

By *that*, Jason assumed Bern meant autoerotic asphyxiation. "Other people's sex lives," he remarked in a what-can-you-do tone.

"Exactly," Bern said. "But the alternative would be even harder to believe, so…" He shrugged.

"You can't think of anyone who might have had a grudge against Ono? Real or perceived?"

"No. Not really. I mean… She could be somewhat irascible. But we all have that coworker. That person who just has to make the day a little harder than it needs to be. That was Ono. You don't kill people for being tiresome."

"Tiresome," Jason repeated thoughtfully.

"That wasn't kind. The truth is, she was a good person and a good instructor." He sighed, and in that weary exhalation was a long history of hanging on to his patience.

"But not good enough to receive tenure?"

"Tenure is increasingly rare and highly competitive." Bern sounded just the littlest bit defensive. "Georgie knew her stuff. No question. When it came to anything to do with film noir or hard-boiled detective films of the twentieth century, her knowledge was *unparalleled*. But."

"But?"

"Knowing a thing and teaching a thing are two different…things. If you follow."

"Those who can, do, and those who can't, teach?"

Bern's lip curled. "First of all, most *can't*, period. Neither do the thing *nor* teach the thing. Secondly, despite the current popularity of homeschooling, not everyone is qualified or capable of teaching. Teaching is itself an art. It requires more than having attended school twenty years earlier."

"I'm not arguing," Jason said. "Especially after the morning I've had."

Bern laughed shortly. "Yes. Well, first...do no harm."

"All the more incentive to wrap this up."

Bern unbent a little. "Georgie was knowledgeable and articulate, but communication, especially when the objective is to *teach*, requires more. She wasn't patient. Nor was she particularly empathetic. Or imaginative. Believe it or not, those traits are just as important—maybe more so—than broad knowledge or a wide vocabulary."

"I see."

Bern groaned. "I'm doing the very thing I didn't want to do, which is speak ill of the dead."

"I don't consider your objective assessment speaking ill of Professor Ono. You're not the first person to suggest she could be difficult."

"Not difficult enough to warrant killing her, if that's actually what happened. Which again, I *don't* believe." Bern threw another harassed look at the clock. "I apologize. I don't mean to rush you, but I've got a lunch meeting."

"Just one more question."

"Shoot."

"Did Professor Ono mention anything to you about locating a print of a rare or lost film?"

Bern looked startled. "No. What film?"

"I don't know."

"You don't…"

Jason shook his head. "According to her grandfather, Professor Ono believed she'd discovered the existence of a film previously believed to be lost."

"There are a *lot* of lost films out there." Bern seemed to gaze inward. "Given that we're talking about Georgie, we're presumably talking about some kind of crime film. You don't know anything more?"

"I believe Ono mentioned a detective film."

Bern's eyes blazed with sudden fanatical light. "*My God.* What if she managed to find one of the three lost Charlie Chan films?" His excitement faded as quickly as it sparked. "No. No, she'd have told me if she'd actually found something like that."

"I understand she belonged to a private film club for collectors."

Bern shrugged. "I wouldn't be surprised. I also wouldn't have any information. She must have belonged to any number of film-related social organizations." He looked at the clock again and rose. "I'm sorry. I really do have to leave. We can continue this later if you—"

Jason rose. "No, I think we're good for now. Thanks for your time."

"Until this is resolved, it's a cloud hanging over all of us. I'll make every effort to see that you have access to whatever you need for your investigation."

"Thank you. I appreciate that."

They shook hands, and Jason headed for the door.

As he stepped into the narrow, shadowy corridor, he spotted Pop a few offices down, oiling the hinges of a door. Pop seemed slightly out of breath for such a non-strenuous task.

He gave Jason a long look, the thick lenses giving his face a blank, opaque expression.

Jason nodded pleasantly.

It was impossible to know for sure, but he couldn't help suspecting Pop had been listening at Bern's office door.

CHAPTER NINE

"I think I've already figured it out," Alex said. "You're investigating Georgie Ono's death."

Jason smiled wryly, picked up his glass. "Good guess."

He'd been to the Tuck Room Tavern a few times, and he'd always liked the idiosyncratic sports-bar-meets-Alice-in-Wonderland vibe. Fancy animal portraits hung over green booths, and enormous diamond-shaped chandeliers illuminated pillars of animal mosaics made from books. A bank of TV screens glowed over the glittering rows of liquor bottles so that patrons could conveniently shout insults at their favorite teams from the bar itself.

Alex had been waiting when Jason arrived, and they were now seated in a snug booth near the windows overlooking the busy street outside. Alex, dressed in calculatedly ripped jeans and a black Orca in Japan woodblock T-shirt, was drinking a pickle jalapeño whiskey sour. Jason played it safe with the Fear.Movie.Lions Double IPA.

Alex said, "Not really. I can't think of anything else in UCLA's recent history that might grab the attention of the FBI Art Crimes Team."

"I'm not sure Ono's death qualifies either," Jason admitted.

"Really? I figured..." Alex let that go.

"What?"

Alex shrugged. "I don't know. It's just a rumor. A while back, she supposedly went to the FBI over something suspish."

"Suspish?"

"Suspicious." Alex's guileless blue gaze met Jason's. "Maybe something to do with film piracy?"

"Where did you hear that?"

Alex looked vague. "I'm not sure, but I don't think Georgie was shy about sharing that kind of information." He sipped his drink.

Jason considered Alex dispassionately. He liked him, and he was Charlotte's friend and client. It wasn't unusual for people to conceal information from law enforcement, and the fact that Alex was hedging didn't mean anything more than he wasn't comfortable blabbing to the feds.

"Did you know Georgie well?"

"No. And I don't have any opinion on whether her death was accidental, suicide, or, I guess now, murder. I just know when my time comes, I don't want cops and reporters snooping through my life."

"Amen." On that, Jason could wholeheartedly agree.

Alex regarded him for a moment, gave a funny smile. "You really do look different. I couldn't believe it was you when I saw you this morning."

"Not different enough." Jason was rueful.

"It's your eyes. You have really striking green eyes." Alex added, "I spent a lot of time gazing into them the night of your birthday party."

"Aw. Shucks." Alex was handsome, smart, and good company. No way was he sitting home Friday nights mourning what-could-have-beens.

"Hey. No lie."

Jason figured they had best stick to business. "There's no indication of murder. The family's still struggling to accept the coroner's verdict. I'm hoping I can reassure them that there were no irregularities in the investigation and no shortcuts."

Alex looked unconvinced. "People are going to believe what they want to believe, right?"

"To an extent. But it was their idea—well, the grandfather's idea—to bring the Bureau in."

"He's a former senator? I guess that carries some clout."

"He's still got some clout," Jason conceded.

Alex took another sip, said, "It's weird to think someone you know was murdered."

Tell me about it. Equally weird to think someone wanted you dead. Not that Kyser necessarily wanted Jason dead. It was hard to know what he *did* want. Safe to say, nothing good.

"So again," Jason was painstaking on this point, "there's no indication that Georgie Ono's death was a homicide."

"But you've only started the investigation."

"There was a thorough investigation after her death. This is largely a courtesy to the family."

"An FBI investigation seems especially courteous." Alex's bright blue eyes studied Jason with curiosity.

Jason shrugged. "Georgie's grandfather was a two-term senator."

"Our paths didn't cross a lot. Different faculties. She wasn't popular. I can tell you that much."

"No?"

"No."

"I heard a group of students were trying to sue her over the LGBTQ content of one of her courses."

"Right. The Celluloid Closet. A title she cribbed from the film, by the way. But despite that bullshit lawsuit, she wasn't particularly controversial."

"She's been described to me as a difficult personality."

"Definitely." Alex met Jason's gaze. "She was opinionated and outspoken."

"That can't be a rarity on a college campus."

"No, but a lot of her opinions were not popular ones. Were not socially approved by the interest groups who would, in theory, be expected to support her."

"*Ah.* Like?"

"She was pretty conservative. Politically, not socially. She had no hesitation bringing her views into the classroom."

"Again, that's the college experience, isn't it? Being exposed to different viewpoints. Ono expressing her political and social views can't have come as a novelty."

"True. The thing is, we live in a social media world, and she was actively hostile to the idea of social media. In particular—well, according to legend—answering a cell phone once you walked through the door of her classroom was an automatic fail."

Cell phones weren't social media. Alex had changed course mid-sentence. Was he referring to Ono's online squabbles on gaming sites and discussion forums? Or something else?

"Social media like YouTube?" Jason suggested.

Alex sipped his cocktail. "Probably."

"YouTube because of its historic role in film piracy?"

"Georgie was outspoken on the subject of piracy, sure." Alex's tone was carefully neutral. "But you already know that." It was part question, part fishing. Alex was right to assume Jason would have heard all about Ono's accusations against Eli Humphrey.

"Sure. I know she published a couple of papers on the connection between film piracy, organized crime, and terrorism."

"I can't say it's a conversation we ever had. In my opinion, cams—bootlegs—played an important role in film preservation. But honestly, in the larger scheme of things, I think the real problem was Georgie had a messy personal life which overflowed into her professional life. That gave the administration ammunition to go after her."

Why would they want to? But Jason didn't ask the obvious question. He had other avenues to pursue that information. Alex had brought up a much more intriguing line of inquiry.

"It does sound like her relationships were complicated. Did you ever meet the girlfriend?"

"The indie director with the lungs of an opera singer?"

"Huh?"

"Not formally. She crashed into me once when she was fleeing Georgie's office. They'd been having a screaming match that made Bette v. Joan sound like a tea party."

Bette v. Joan? Oh. *Whatever Happened to Baby Jane.*

"But you must know Professor Bardolf?"

"Balthasar?" Alex's smile was sardonic. "Oh yeah. I know BB pretty well. What did you think of him?"

Jason recognized the attempt to divert the conversation, but also knew Alex was getting tired of being questioned and starting to regret agreeing to meet.

"I haven't met him yet."

"You're kidding. He probably knew Georgie better than anyone. Seriously. If you want to know about Georgie, he's the guy to talk to."

"I plan to. They were together a long time?"

"Define together." Alex grimaced. "I think it was one of those can't-live-with-'em-can't-live-without-'em relationships." He added hastily, "BB is *not* a violent guy. I don't mean that."

"Right. Sure," Jason said easily.

"You should know he can come off a little arrogant. If he's feeling defensive."

"I'll keep that in mind."

"But he really knows his stuff."

"Does he?"

"Oh, hell yeah. He worked on the 4K restorations of *Gun Crazy* and *The Big Shakedown*. Oh, and *Murder in Harlem*. Crime films are his specialty. If you can get him going on the topic of film noir, he's actually pretty good company."

"Crime films were Georgie's specialty too?"

"That's right." Alex raised his glass in a half toast. "Their life of crime brought them together."

They talked a little while longer. Jason declined another drink. Wilshire, the backbone of Los Angeles, was always crowded, and at this time of the evening it would take at least half an hour to get over to Koreatown and find a place to park. The indie director with the lungs of an opera singer had made it very clear tardiness was not acceptable. He did not want an aria on the topic of being late.

Alex insisted on picking up the tab, which Jason suspected was about not wanting to feel his information had been bought and paid for.

"Thanks for the drink. Can I ask a favor? Can I ask you to keep my identity confidential?"

Alex, tucking his credit card into the leather server book, smiled cynically. "I knew *that* was coming."

"It's important, or I wouldn't ask."

Alex considered. He sighed. "To be honest, I've been trying to make my mind up. I don't want to have to lie to friends or colleagues."

"I understand."

Alex's gaze was troubled. "But for now, yes, I'll keep your identity confidential."

Jason didn't try to hide his relief. "Thank you. I mean that."

Alex shrugged it off. "By the way, are you still dating that flinty profiler?"

Jason couldn't help the instinctive smile at the thought of Sam. "I am. Yes."

"That's a shame."

Jason winked. "Thanks, but I can't agree."

Sunset fell around eight o'clock this time of the year, but the light was already changing, turning soft and pensive. The summer air was dry and warm and laced with the usual Los Angeles fragrance of smog and tar and night-blooming jasmine. It was less than a minute's walk to the parking structure where Jason had left his car. He had plenty to think over. What Alex hadn't said had been as interesting as what he had. Though he'd skirted the topic of film piracy, he obviously knew Ono had filed a report with the FBI accusing film collector Eli Humphrey of piracy—and he clearly had not been on Team Ono.

Understandable if Alex felt conflicted. The FBI raids in the 1970s of high-profile film collectors like Roddy McDowall and Woody Wise were still a sore spot with cinephiles. Film buffs with the foresight to preserve what the studios at the time considered disposable had been harassed and prosecuted by those very studios once they realized their error. The studios had the money and influence to recreate history, and unfortunately, in that endeavor the FBI and other law enforcement agencies had too often acted as corporate lackeys.

The raids were now largely considered a mistake. Not only had most of the charges ultimately been dropped, harassment of innocent collectors had made the collecting community as a whole far less likely to cooperate with the authorities when it came to genuine pirates and pirating.

Being on the wrong side of film preservation—let alone history—was not a thought that gave Jason a lot of pleasure.

Another thought that did not give him pleasure was the realization that Alex might be more involved in his case than he'd anticipated.

He retrieved his car and was just turning onto Wilshire when J.J. phoned, greeting him with a cheerful, "Hey, I heard you almost got wiped out last night?"

"What?"

"That near collision over Wilshire. The 747 nearly hit your apartment building."

"*Oh*, right."

"Don't tell me you slept through *that*?"

"No. No, I woke up for that. It's just been a long day."

"I bet. Speaking of. How *was* your first day of school?"

Was there maybe just a *hint* of glee in J.J.'s undertone? Bastard.

"I'm gonna need a bigger box of throat lozenges."

J.J.'s tone grew reminiscent. "It should be a dream come true for you, West. Hours and *hours* of droning on to one captive audience after another. Those sleep-deprived youngsters are finally going to catch up on their rest."

"Hey. They were hanging on my every word. They'll never burn another illegal copy of a CD again."

"*Riiight.* Speaking of bullshit, how *are* you going to fake teaching a bunch of college-level courses?"

"I'm not worried about that."

J.J. began to splutter.

"I give seminars all the time on protecting and preserving art collections. It's not that much different."

"Uh, yeah. Keep telling yourself that. Do you know anything about film or film studies?"

"More than I did at this time last night. Anyway, I have Dahle's lesson plan to follow."

"Show them a movie. That's what our substitutes always did."

"I've already got the entire junior varsity napping in my back row."

J.J. said sincerely, "Those poor kids."

Jason laughed. "You're an asshole. Is there a point to this phone call, or did you just want to savor my misery?"

"Why can't it be both?" J.J.'s tone changed. "But okay, you know how I thought this was a total waste of our time?"

"How could I forget?"

"It turns out, maybe Grandpa isn't totally delusional."

"You found something?"

"You don't have to sound so surprised."

Jason, nudging his way into the slow-moving train of traffic, grinned. "Sorry." The driver of the car parallel to his flipped him off. Jason, fluent in the dialect of inner-city driving, absently flicked his middle finger in answer. "What have you got?"

"The month before Ono died, she reported two separate attempts to break into her apartment."

Jason stopped smiling, glancing instinctively at his messenger bag. "There's no mention of that anywhere in her case file."

"She didn't report it to the cops or even to campus security. She reported it to Touchstone's onsite security service."

"Why the hell, after her death, didn't *they* report it to the cops?"

"Cutting through the corporate-speak, they didn't believe her. Or claim they didn't believe her. And since her death was clearly not homicide, it was irrelevant."

"Part of why her death was not investigated as a homicide would be the withholding of that kind of evidence!"

"I know. There might have been an interterritorial pissing match going on."

"Fucking fantastic."

"There's more."

Jason said tersely, "Go on."

"The week before Ono died, she filed a sexual harassment complaint against one of the security guards. Oh, sorry, *officers*."

"Are you kidding me? What happened with that?"

"Dismissed for lack of evidence."

"*What?*"

J.J.'s said grimly, "Once again, they didn't believe her. In fact, according to Dennis Rice, Touchstone's Chief of Security, Professor Ono was a very troubled lady who would do pretty much anything for attention."

"For God's sake."

Two complaints filed over Ono's belief someone was trying to get into her apartment. Then a charge of sexual harassment. With three complaints dismissed by the head of building security, had Ono taken her concerns to the property management company? She didn't seem like someone who would accept being blown off.

Of course, she might not have realized she was being blown off.

Or there might be another reason why she hadn't elevated her complaint. Maybe she *was* making stuff up for attention.

J.J. said, "My thought."

"What is?"

"That there might be some liability in Ono's death on the part of Touchstone."

Jason said slowly, "Do we know which security guard she accused of harassment?"

"Not yet." J.J.'s tone was grim. "We will."

Jason stared unseeingly at the never-ending twilight land-scape of apartment buildings and skyscrapers. The question mark curve of towering streetlamps and glowing neon signs offering quick solutions: cocktails, clubs, cinema.

...moaning from close-up kisses, black-and-white kisses that could not be felt.

"None of this came up in my interview with the senator. Which, you'd think it would, given that it supports the family's theory of foul play."

"Maybe she didn't tell him. Maybe she did make it up."

"Maybe." Was that possible? Ono had a reputation for filing complaints over things most people would let slide. Had she viewed an off-color comment as a firing offense? Was this a case of crying wolf, or was there something legit here?

"Anyway," J.J. sounded uncharacteristically diffident, "I'd like to take point on this line of inquiry."

Well, hell. The first genuinely promising lead they'd had, and J.J. had uncovered it. Jason struggled with himself for a second or two.

"Yeah, of course. It's your lead, Russell."

"How's it going on your end? Have you learned anything?"

Jason said wearily, "Yes. Teachers aren't paid *nearly* enough."

J.J. surprised him by sharing, "My sister teaches junior high. You couldn't pay me enough to walk into a room of junior high schoolers."

"Hostage situations are always dangerous," Jason deadpanned. He brought J.J. up to speed on his own discoveries, such as they were.

"Your cover's *already* blown?" J.J. was exasperated.

"It wasn't much of a cover."

"I'll say!"

"In fairness, it wasn't meant to be deep cover."

"Is this ex-boyfriend going to go around blabbing that you're an FBI agent?"

"He's not an ex-boyfriend, and I hope not. He says not. I don't know him well enough to predict."

"This is all we needed."

"It's not a great start, but it sounds like if there was anything suspish about Ono's death, it happened on her home turf."

"Suspish?"

"Suspicious."

J.J. was silent.

"Destination arrived," Jason said, pulling onto Catalina Street and spotting the valet parking for Intercrew. "I'll touch base tomorrow."

"Yeah. Hey, West?"

"Mm?"

"Don't trust the ex-boyfriend. It's a weird coincidence, his knowing our victim. I don't like coincidences."

CHAPTER TEN

Calida Lois was a small, stocky Blasian woman in a tight black skirt, white tube top, and a black hat with ball fringe. She had spectacular teeth, which she brandished at Jason in a not-exactly-a-smile, and eyeliner Cleopatra would have envied. But then she was what was still known in SoCal as *in the business*. The business being movie making. People in the business were never off, which was probably why they were meeting in trendy, glam Intercrew versus somewhere they could actually talk.

Or maybe not talking was the point.

Or maybe Lois just really liked the Anejo honey sour cocktails.

"You're late," she informed Jason.

It was exactly one minute to eight, but Jason said, "Thank you so much for waiting." He took a chair across the table from the blue banquette where she sat.

The restaurant was huge. A sobriety test of a marble staircase led down to a moodily lit maze of low couches and tables and chairs. Chandeliers that looked like deadly ice sculptures hung from towering ceilings. The music—K-Pop—was deafening. Every seat in the place was taken.

Lois extended a small hand with long pearl-colored nails. It was not in greeting. "Credentials."

Jason handed over his credentials, and Lois spent a full minute studying his ID. At last, she handed back the leather badge holder. "You don't look like an FBI agent."

"We don't all look alike."

Lois's eyes narrowed, but then she laughed. It was an attention-grabbing laugh, but seemed genuine.

"That's a good one. Let's order because it can take forever when they're busy—and they're always busy."

"Sure."

Their server appeared right on cue, and Lois started with the Astrea caviar at one hundred and forty-five dollars a pop and a bottle of Red Car Estate chardonnay at one hundred and twenty-three. Jason pictured what George Potts would have to say about his expense report and ordered a Kamikaze.

Under the mellowing effect of good wine and caviar served on toasted baguettes with sunshine eggs and crème fraîche, Lois unbent a little.

"So, in answer to your question, no, I did not kill Georgie."

"That wasn't my question," Jason said. "Professor Ono's death was ruled accidental."

"Yeah, and I'm up for an Academy Award. I know *exactly* what *you're* about, Mr. F. B. I."

About three hundred dollars including tax, and they still hadn't ordered dinner.

Jason tried to reassure her. "Professor Ono's family is having trouble coming to terms with her death. I'm hoping

I can bring a little closure by helping them understand what happened."

Lois arched against the back of the blue banquette, cackling. "Right. They just can't figure it out! Like they don't have any part in this."

"You think it was suicide?"

"It sure as hell wasn't *accidental*. My girl never had an *accident* in her life."

"I spo—"

Lois cut in, "And she sure as fuck didn't *accidentally* strangubate herself."

"Okay. You knew her. Why would she kill herself?"

Lois raised her chin, said haughtily, "Maybe she killed herself over me."

"Did she?"

"No." She reached for her wineglass. Her smile was odd. "She wasn't that invested. Not in me. Not in anyone else either."

"Then, again, why would she kill herself?"

Lois swallowed a mouthful of wine, considered, said, "Whilst the balance of her mind was disturbed. That's what they say in those old movies, right?"

"I guess so. But what would have disturbed the balance of her mind to such an extent? The argument with you?"

Lois laughed, but this time it was quiet and a little bitter. "No. I was the one trying to get back together that night. She didn't care. I was crying, and she was *bored*. That's why—" She cut herself off.

Jason said, "The discussion turned physical?"

She curled her lip. *"Turned physical.* You could call it that. Have you ever sobbed your heart out to someone and had them sit there like a stone, like they're wondering if they remembered to set the DVR?"

It hadn't been quite that bad, but Jason could relate. There was no one stonier than Sam when he shut off. He made a non-committal noise.

"I wanted to shake her into showing she felt something. But I just scared her." Lois said wearily, "I scared myself."

Jason began, "She had a lot of bad news in a short amount of time—" but was interrupted by the server arriving to take entrée orders.

Lois ordered the Australian Wagyu Tomahawk—on-the-bone ribeye steak imported from Japan—with romesco and horseradish cream, and priced at a gulp-inducing two hundred and seventy dollars. Jason went for the spicy Sichuan fried chicken and summoned another Kamikaze posthaste.

As their server vanished into the crowd, Lois said, "Not getting tenure was bullshit. She was right to take that personally because that was absolutely payback."

"Payback for what?"

"The previous year she'd filed a complaint with the administration, stating she'd experienced chronic operational and procedural problems amid a contentious and distrustful work environment. You can imagine how much that was appreciated."

"I'm guessing things got a little awkward?" Jason suggested.

"To say the least. But before you discount what I'm telling you because other people are telling you how *difficult* Georgie was, she wasn't alone in her feelings. That film school is famous for low morale among its faculty, staff, and students."

"Is it?"

"It is. And she wasn't the first to try to bring the situation to the administration's attention. Or the last. When the school's Academic Senate concluded their eight-year review, they noted serious grievances coming from the student body as well. The dog-eat-dog attitude in the faculty ranks is an open secret."

"So, you believe the unfairness of the administration's decision drove Georgie to take her own life?"

Lois hesitated, admitted, "It wouldn't have been that alone."

Alex's theory on why Ono had not received tenure boiled down to squeamishness on the part of the administration following a high-profile lawsuit. He wasn't sure if Lois's hypothesis was the more likely. In fact, he suspected these things combined had factored against Ono.

"When you heard the accidental-death verdict, what was your first thought?"

"No way."

"You thought suicide made more sense?"

"No. No way."

Jason opened his mouth, but Lois broke in with a heartfelt, "Neither makes sense. But the alternative doesn't make sense either. Georgie would never open her door to a stranger."

It wouldn't have been a stranger, of course. It would have been someone who knew Ono. Knew her well enough to set her death scene with those particular props. Someone who knew her intimately. Someone she trusted.

As if reading his thoughts, Lois said, "Anyway, there are security cameras all over that building, so if they didn't capture anyone…"

"Because of a perceived lack of available storage space, at that time Touchstone's video surveillance system only archived for forty-eight hours. Georgie's body wasn't discovered until the relevant footage had been recorded over."

"I didn't know that. Oh my God." Lois's hand shook as she refilled her wineglass. "Have you spoken to Bardolf?"

"Not yet."

"You need to talk to him. But don't believe anything he tells you."

Jason raised his brows. "Everything I hear, I take with a grain of salt."

For instance, Lois had begun their conversation by denying her own involvement in Ono's possible homicide, throwing shade on Ono's family, then suggesting factors including run-ins with the administration might have led to suicide, and now, finally, she was hinting that her romantic rival, Professor Bardolf, might hold the answers.

The only thing Jason was sure of was that Lois's feelings for Georgette Ono were possessive and passionate and had led to at least one physical altercation.

He asked, "Did Georgie tell you she believed she'd dis-covered a possibly valuable lost film?"

Lois frowned. "That fell through."

"It did?"

"I think it did. Last I heard, it did. Georgie said she'd finally got the money together—God knows how because she was always broke—but the seller changed their mind. Georgie was sick about it. She was really counting on getting her hands on that print. That's a book that *would* have sold."

Still more bad news for Georgie. Did this provide another motive for suicide?

Jason said only, "Did she mention who the seller was?"

"She was careful *not* to mention who the seller was, but obviously it was someone on campus."

"Why obviously?"

"Well, I mean, from the way she spoke, it seemed to me it had to be someone she saw fairly regularly. I just assumed."

"She belonged to some kind of film club, didn't she? Could—"

"No. They kicked her out after she went to the police about Eli Humphrey. But yeah, it's possible, I guess."

A little confusing, but he thought he followed. "Did she tell you what the film was?"

Lois shook her head. "I know it was supposed to be a film noir from the 1950s, which rules out all the missing Chan and Holmes films. I know it was supposedly American-made, which eliminates *The Diamond*. The problem is, there aren't any known missing crime or mystery films from the '50s to fit that description. Which I told her."

"You think it was a scam?"

"I think it must have been. But Georgie knew her detective films, so there was *something* there for her to get excited about. Maybe a screenplay exists? Or she was shown some outtakes or publicity stills? My guess is the film was never actually made."

"But Georgie didn't think it was a scam?"

"No. She was one hundred percent convinced she had found a lost noir masterpiece."

Jason was thinking out loud. "If it *was* a scam, why didn't the seller carry through with the scheme?"

"My take? Georgie was *not* someone you'd want to try to scam. She'd have gone straight to the cops, whether she implicated herself in wrongdoing or not." Lois's laugh was short and harsh. "Hell, even if that film existed, if she decided there was something suspect in how it was acquired, she might have gone to the police. She could be a little bit…fanatical."

That certainly sounded like the Georgette Ono who was taking shape in Jason's imagination.

If the person attempting to sell Ono this purported lost film was someone she dealt with on a regular basis, surely they'd known her proclivity for going to the authorities before ever reaching out to her?

The question remained: why had they backed out?

Jason had to wait until Lois finished ordering dessert—Basque cheesecake for an inconsequential fourteen dollars—to ask, "When did this deal fall through? Do you know?"

Lois shook her head, and the little black balls on her hat swayed back and forth. "We weren't seeing each other. Georgie mentioned in passing that last evening that it had fallen through." She added bleakly, "It was obvious she cared more about losing an imaginary film than losing me."

CHAPTER ELEVEN

A thousand dollars later—give or take that twenty-percent tip—Jason let himself into Ono's apartment.

He slid the deadbolt, found the entrance hall light switch, all the while still speaking on his cell.

"Hey, we said we'd talk later, but I just wanted to say, I know this is—isn't easy. The news about Berkle's possible accomplice." He added awkwardly—because even after everything they'd been through, these types of conversations did not come naturally with Sam, "I'm thinking of you. That's all."

For God's sake. *I'm thinking of you?* Why stop there? Why not send one of those singing e-cards. He looked at his cell screen trying to remember if there was any possible way to delete a phone message after you'd okayed it, but paused at the heavy knock on the door behind him.

A glance through the peephole offered the fish-eyed vision of a scowling Hugo Quintana.

"What the hell is your deal?" Jason muttered. He plastered on a pleasant smile and jerked open the door. "Yep?"

"Hanging items on or from any balcony violates the terms of your lease."

"Huh?"

"You've got a beach towel hanging from the bedroom balcony. You can't do that."

Jason said, "I'm not hanging anything from the balcony."

"Your beach towel is visible to everyone."

"My—" Jason automatically glanced over his shoulder. The living room balcony was empty of so much as a hanging plant, let alone a beach towel. "Hang on a minute."

He closed the door, locked it, and immediately Quintana began to knock—hard. What. An. Ass. Did he think Jason was making a run for it by rappelling down the side of the building?

Jason strode down the hall, poked his head inside the guest bedroom, and saw…nothing. He headed to the master bedroom, and sure enough—well, not sure enough because there was no beach towel, but there *was* a large violet and blue delta kite draped over the balcony like a huge broken wing. The kite's snapped line had somehow snagged between the Plexiglas wall and stainless-steel railing.

Jason stepped outside the air-conditioned bedroom into the humid warmth of the evening. He spared a glance for the river of headlights winding through the city streets thirty stories down. Luckily, he didn't have a problem with heights, but Sam wouldn't care for this view. So far, discomfort with heights was the only weakness Sam had confided.

It took a minute or two to untangle the very long kite line, which whipped around in the breeze. He could hear the distant roar of traffic, the *hum* of air conditioners, and the bickering of the couple in the apartment below over who was supposed to pay the Netflix subscription.

No lie, it was a *long* way down.

At last, he had the line free. He carried the bundle of polyester and fiberglass poles to the kitchen, examining it briefly just in case there was a message or a threat written on the shiny material. He felt silly, especially when there was nothing there. He left the bundle on the floor and went to answer the door, which Quintana was still pounding on.

As he opened the door, Quintana demanded, "Is there some reason you don't want me inside this apartment?"

"Is that a trick question?" Jason asked. "No, I don't want you inside. Anyway, it wasn't a beach towel. A kite got caught on the railing."

Somehow this innocent explanation triggered greater suspicion on the part of Touchstone's security officer. "How would that happen?"

"I couldn't tell you. At a guess, some kid was flying a kite and the line snapped."

"That doesn't sound very likely."

Jason sighed. "It's more likely than me spending time at the pool or going to the beach. If you'd like the kite for evidence, I'm happy to hand it over."

Quintana was unamused.

"You have a good evening," Jason told him, and closed the door once more.

Quintana did not like him. Did not trust him. That didn't mean Quintana himself was untrustworthy or up to no good. Safe to say, Touchstone's entire security team would be on the defense these days.

He was staring down at the kite, wondering if its unlikely presence on his balcony had been some sort of ruse to get into the apartment—which would not make sense, given that anyone who planted the kite would surely already have access to the apartment—when Sam's number flashed up.

Jason mentally replayed the message he'd left just a little while earlier, groaned, and answered his cell.

"Hey," he said apologetically.

"Hey. What was that about? That message you just left."

"I just… I realized I was pretty…oblivious yesterday."

Sam said almost cautiously, "Were you?"

"I know this situation with Berkle has to be difficult for a bunch of reasons."

"Yes. It's frustrating we overlooked the obvious." Sam was brisk and all business. "We can focus on our mistakes, or we can work to make up the lost ground. This time last year we didn't have anything. So."

That wasn't what Jason meant at all, but he understood that Sam didn't want to get into the personal implications for himself in the Roadside Ripper case. He respected Sam's feelings, even if Sam didn't want to acknowledge he had feelings.

Jason said doubtfully, "So everything's okay?"

"Everything's under control," Sam said.

"Is that the same as okay?" Jason was only partly kidding.

Sam said with that note of indulgence he got sometimes, "Everything's okay, West. You don't have to worry."

"I do worry about you. Believe it or not."

"I know." Sam hesitated, said, "It's…nice."

Jason smiled, wishing not for the first time—and definitely not for the last—that the nearly entire continental United States did not lie between them.

Sam said briskly, "How's the case coming?"

"I'm still trying to decide if there *is* a case."

"Meaning?"

Jason sighed. "I wish I knew. It's the weirdest thing. I can't, for the life of me, get a handle on who my victim was. I'm living in her apartment, surrounded by her books and papers, but she's still a cipher. I've interviewed her friends, family, even the UCPD detective who originally caught the case, and they all seem to be describing a person they didn't know that well either. Maybe I'm not asking the right questions. Maybe I'm out of practice."

"You want me to take a look at the case file?"

"*No.*" Jason's instant, instinctive rejection hung in the air like the echo of a slammed door. He tried to soften it. "Thanks, but I know how busy you are."

"Being busy is my job." Jason didn't have to see Sam's face to know he was frowning.

"Right. But we don't have an offender to profile. I'm not even sure our victim *is* a victim."

He could feel Sam weighing his words. "The BAU doesn't just profile offenders. Every investigation begins by analyzing and interpreting the behaviors and interactions of the victim. You know that."

"Yes. I know."

"We receive requests from federal, state, local, and international law enforcement agencies every day. Why would I not have time to look at *your* case file?"

"Sam." Just as Sam was trying not to show his impatience, Jason was doing his best not to let exasperation creep into his tone. "I was thinking out loud, not filing a request for help."

"West, if you need help—"

"I don't. I was just…bitching to my boyfriend."

There was a sharp silence. Sam said quietly, "This is about Montana."

"It really isn't." But yeah, it really was. *Of course* it was. Jason was never going to willingly ask Sam for help again, and he knew it wasn't logical or fair or maybe even smart, but a part of him couldn't quite get past the experience of going to sleep believing Sam would find a way through the quagmire, only to wake up and face Sam's icy rage and contempt.

It wasn't that Jason didn't trust Sam. He blamed himself for all of it. But he would never again risk their relationship by asking too much from Sam.

He said quickly, lightly, "If I really do need help, you'll hear about it. In triplicate. I promise."

Another of those very loud silences before Sam said, "That's a promise I'll hold you to."

That wasn't a social pleasantry. Sam meant exactly what he said, and Jason's heart sank. Why was Sam so goddamned literal about everything?

He said, "Hey, I've got a long day tomorrow. I should go. I…love you."

Sam absorbed the fact that they would not be speaking later in the evening, said without hesitation or inflection, "I love you too." Uncompromising as always.

Jason thought of—and discarded—a couple of responses, but in the end left it alone and clicked off.

He didn't sleep well.

Thirty-one stories up, the wind pushed against the floor-to-ceiling windows and whispered outside the glass doors. Jason's dreams went from bad to worse, and he woke, heart pounding, drenched in sweat, with Jeremy Kyser's weird, sing-songy, *"Agent West?"* ringing in his ears.

He knew where he was. Knew he was perfectly safe.

Yet it was all he could do not to reach for his Glock. All he could do not to turn on a lamp. It turned into a battle of will, lying there in the dark, listening to the building sway and moan. He was not going to give in to irrational fear. He was not going to let Kyser control his life. Not in the big things. Not in the little things.

Which didn't change that he'd give a lot to know where Kyser was right at this minute.

The important thing was he was *not* standing on the balcony outside this room.

So…get a grip, West.

Jason punched his pillow and did what he usually did when he couldn't sleep. Well, one of the things he usually did. In this instance, it was to run over the details of his case.

He kept coming back to his victim.

The one thing everyone seemed to agree on was that Georgette Ono was difficult.

The other thing everyone—with the understandable exception of Touchstone's security team—agreed on was that it was *almost* as hard to believe she'd accidentally killed herself as it was to believe she committed suicide.

The problem was…

Well, there were a number of problems.

One, he was there to reassure the family, not reopen the case. No one wanted a cover-up. But there was also no expectation that Jason was actually going to find anything. In fact, the expectation was the opposite.

If he actually reopened the case, turned it into an active homicide investigation, there would be, at best, a mixed reception from his superiors.

Two, even if he privately believed Ono was the victim of homicide, he had no real suspect and no real motive.

Even if LAPD had failed to discover Ono's allegedly contentious relationship with Touchstone's security—which seemed unlikely, since the head of security apparently had no issue in sharing that info with J.J.—it didn't feel like enough of a motive.

Speculation was going to make it harder, not easier, on the Ono family.

Three—and this had nothing to do with his case—he felt like with each phone call, he and Sam were getting further apart. They were both reasonably articulate, they both wanted this relationship to work, so what was going on?

Was it just him, or was it Sam too? He honestly wasn't sure.

"Hell," Jason muttered and reached for his cell, peering at the screen.

Just after two, which meant Sam might be asleep. He tended to crash around ten and be up and running—literally—by four. Jason tried not to interrupt those few precious hours when Sam allowed himself the luxury of turning off, but tonight…

Tonight, the distance between them was harder to take than usual.

He struggled with himself for a minute or two, then pressed Sam's number.

Sam answered on the half-ring. "Hey." He sounded wide awake, his voice as soft as if they were lying facing each other. "Bad dreams?"

Jason let out a long breath he hadn't realized he was holding. "No. I didn't like the way we left things tonight."

"Me neither." No hesitation. It was like Sam had been lying there thinking the same.

"The thing about trying to make this work long distance is…not letting stuff pile up."

He could feel Sam thinking that over. "What's piling up, Jason?"

Jason, not West. Jason considered that demarcation. Considered the careful gravity of Sam's voice.

"I want to make sure you don't get the wrong idea. It's not that I don't—"

"Trust me?" Sam sounded dry.

"Yes. It's not that I don't trust you."

"What is it, then? Because there's something."

"It's a fine line for both of us. That's the lesson of Montana. You're not just another agent. You're a unit chief. There are potential conflicts."

"That might hold water if you were in my unit." No give. No leeway.

"Okay, let's call it priorities."

Sam said crisply, "You're my priority."

Jason gave a shaky laugh. "Well, wait a minute, because that's not accurate. It's not even the agreement we made. It's not my expectation."

He could hear the shrug in Sam's voice. "Nor was it mine, but that's the way it's playing out."

Did Sam really believe that? He was no liar, so yeah, he believed what he was saying. But what he was saying was not an accurate reflection of, well, you name it. It certainly didn't reflect Jason's experience.

"Since when?"

Once again there was that uncharacteristic wry note in Sam's tone. "Probably since the morning you arrived at my hotel door barefoot, hair dripping, hollering how dare I phone SAC Manning about your fitness for duty."

At the time, they'd known each other less than twenty-four hours. Now it felt like a million years ago.

"Hey, I never said *how dare you.*"

"Maybe not those exact words." Sam actually sounded amused at the memory. "You were highly offended."

Was Sam really implying he'd started to fall for Jason the morning after they'd met? For Jason, the awareness had been instant, the attraction had followed against his better judgment, but once he'd fallen, he'd acknowledged it, accepted it. Sam might have been interested and attracted, but he had fought those feelings long and hard. So Jason couldn't help feeling a little skeptical.

Whatever it is you need, Jason, I'm probably not that guy.

"As I recall, the agreement was work would always come first for you and that I was willing to accept that for however long I could."

"We all have our dreams," Sam said. "That one fell by the roadside a long time ago."

He was being ironic, but yeah. True. There was no point in rehashing ancient history. Sam had drawn the rules of engagement. Sam had also been the first to break those rules.

Sam said crisply, "We both made mistakes in Montana. We've both explained and clarified and apologized. Is there anything you need to hear from me that I haven't said?"

"No," Jason answered. Sam had said everything he could. In fairness, he had said everything he needed to say. "Is there anything more you need to hear from me?"

"I'm not the one feeling like I can't confide in my partner."

Partner.

Okay, right there. That word. That was not a word either of them had ever used before. In all honesty, Jason didn't think they were there yet. Yes, the weekend Sam had spent at Jason's bungalow, he'd suggested they move in together. But he had also admitted he wasn't sure it was a great idea and that the offer was largely driven by concern for Jason's welfare.

Not the most persuasive of arguments for sharing a coffeemaker and Pandora passwords.

That said, they *were* on the same track. Sam had articulated what Jason wanted. Jason just needed to be sure Sam wanted it as much as he did and not merely because *WWWD.*

"This isn't the conversation I wanted to have," Jason admitted.

After an alarmingly quiet moment, Sam said, "What does that mean?"

That we're wading into deep water.

Jason struck back toward the safety of the shallows. "That you're right. I've been hesitant to ask for help. That's on me, not you."

After a moment, Sam asked, "Are we past that, or is this still a problem?"

Earlier that evening, Jason had been dead set against asking Sam for help ever again, but that was not rational or reasonable. Sam—the BAU—was a valuable resource. Nor was it fair when Sam was doing his best to make up for his perceived failings.

"We're past it."

He hadn't realized how tense Sam was until he heard the relative lightness of his, "Why don't you tell me about your case?"

Jason sighed and stared out the glass windows at the scattered pinpoints of light. The city was slowly waking up to another day.

"Well, the first thing is, I'm pretty sure it's murder."

CHAPTER TWELVE

On Tuesday morning someone tried to kill him.

Or at least, that was how it seemed at the time.

It was six-thirty, and Jason was coming back from his run. Along with its considerable other amenities, Touchstone's residents had access to a beautifully landscaped one-acre park with flower gardens and water features. His mind was on coffee as he crossed the front driveway parking lot on his way toward the lobby entrance. Should he opt for Starbucks or try the on-site café? Which would be faster this time of the morning?

He absently noted a car engine roaring into life—someone needed a transmission tune-up—and then, seemingly out of nowhere, a battered gold Chevy Impala came hurtling toward him.

"Jesus Christ..." Jason dove toward the large square fountain. He tucked and rolled—never pleasant on stamped concrete—and landed safely. The heat of the car engine and exhaust from its pipes blew past him with inches to spare. The hair on his arms prickled. Bits of grit stung his face.

"You asshole!" Adrenaline pumping, he scrambled up, trying to get the license, but the plate was not there. The vehicle screeched out of the driveway and disappeared into the morning work traffic on Wilshire.

Confusingly, the driver was lying on the horn as though Jason had nearly run *him* over. So *was* it an accident?

A couple of residents and a security guard—not Hugo Quintana—ran over to see if he was okay, and Jason reassured everyone that he was fine, barring some bumps and bruises.

No one had a license number. No one got a clear look at the driver. According to one bystander, the driver had been wearing a Michael Myers Halloween mask. A second bystander had seen an elderly man with binoculars behind the wheel. According to the last witness, a blonde woman on her cell phone had been driving. The security guard had not seen the driver but was certain the car did not belong to a resident.

In other words, bubkes.

The conversation quickly devolved into a debate about whether the auto court should be open to non-residents, and Jason excused himself and went to shower.

He was more mad than shaken. It seemed too early in his investigation for him to have riled anyone to the point of wanting to take him out. And though Jeremy Kyser was never far from his thoughts, Sam had explained that Kyser was unlikely to want him dead. Not right off the bat. Not until Kyser'd had time to explain himself and his manifesto up close and in person.

Which was the good news?

Maybe?

Anyway, despite the uneasy feeling that someone had deliberately tried to run him down, it seemed unlikely. True, two close calls in nearly as many days left Jason feeling a little like there was a target on his back, but just because there was a target on your back didn't mean everyone was out to get you.

He showered, shaved, dressed—every time he glanced in the mirror and saw his reflection, he got a jolt—and headed out to UCLA.

How was it possible that *one* day in, he was already getting reviews?

Did these kids have nothing better to do? Didn't they have homework?

Professor desperately needs to reduce caffeine intake.

Professor talks really fast, goes off on tangents, and loses me.

Auditioning for role as college professor in a sitcom that will be canceled after one season. (Nice ass, though.)

Just when you think you know what he's talking about, you don't.

Jason wasn't sure if he was more irritated with Bern for jovially pointing out the reviews or himself for reading them.

As if his "Rate My Professor's Substitute" scores weren't bad enough, Professor Bardolf spent Tuesdays and Wednesdays at the Stoa facility in Santa Clarita, where the archive now resided. He would not be back on campus until Thursday.

Jason tried to get in touch with Ono's former teaching assistant, but the young man had moved to Vermont.

His request for Ono's personnel records was still "going through the channels."

He spoke to Detective Gil Hickok at LAPD's Art Theft Detail about Ono's accusations against Eli Humphrey.

"Ono. I remember her," Hickok said. "That was a weird one, as I recall."

Hickok—Hick to his friends—didn't just head up ATD. He pretty much *was* ATD. Jason had worked with him on numerous occasions over the past two years, and he liked and trusted Hick.

"How so?"

"Kind of hard to explain. It's not that we don't appreciate the help offered by concerned citizens, but my impression was the professor had an ax to grind. You know the dilemma with these very old films."

Oh yes. Jason knew the dilemma. Some of the existing prints of very old and very rare movies were rescues. Technically, it was not possible to demonstrate ownership because the films had been saved from dumpsters or purchased at swap meets and yard sales or salvaged from old theaters or even taped from late night TV. And being in possession of a film you could not prove ownership of was liable to get you charged with piracy and copyright infringement, depending on what you tried to do with that film.

"My understanding is Ono and Humphrey were both members of some kind of cinephile social club. And that she got kicked out of the club after fingering Humphrey."

Hick sighed. "Yeah, as the investigation proceeded, she wanted us to fix that for her too."

"Oops. That's not how that works." Jason felt an unexpected twinge of sympathy for Professor Ono, who hadn't seemed to understand you couldn't legally force someone to be your friend.

"No. It's not."

"What ax do you think she wanted to grind? Do you know?"

"I could never be sure because, of course, everyone clammed up after we got involved. We ended up handing it off to your guys."

"Right. Where the investigation pretty much hit a wall."

"Yeah. I think the falling out started over her being excluded from a particular screening."

"You're joking."

"I'm not sure, because her story changed after that initial interview. She did seem to feel she had been deliberately left out of, uh, group activities and that Humphrey was in possession of illegal materials."

That was a slightly different take than the story Jason had previously heard. "What kind of illegal materials? Pirated films or something else?"

"Unknown."

A disturbing thought occurred. "Child pornography maybe?"

"I did wonder. But see, that's where it got murky. My impression was we weren't talking about pirated movies, but she wouldn't come right out and say it. Whatever *it* was. Maybe she wasn't one hundred percent sure. But then midway through, we were talking about pirated movies and copyright infringement."

"Are you sure—"

"No," Hick said. "I'm not sure. At first, I had the impression she was scared. But that feeling faded, and I'm not sure I didn't imagine it."

"She burned her boats with that interview. Maybe the realization shook her a little."

"That's a good point," Hick said. "Because her boyfriend was part of the movie club, and after she got over her initial outrage, she started worrying about endangering his position at UCLA. He works as an archivist, and getting wrapped up in a film piracy investigation would not exactly be a career booster."

"He'd lose his job," Jason said. Or would have, pre-tenure.

Hick didn't have much more to add, which left Jason the option of poring over his case files yet again.

Nothing new popped out at him.

Sam's observations the previous evening had been interesting but had not really shed new light on the character and psyche of Georgette Ono.

"Most likely a middle child," Sam had theorized, "but she didn't display the usual degree of peacekeeping and compromise. The opposite, in fact."

"I thought you didn't put credence in birth-order theory?"

"As a whole, I don't. But there are obvious generalities. Your victim is someone with a strong sense of grievance. Proof of emotional investment and atonement for perceived slights will have been constants in her relationships."

"Romantic relationships?"

"All relationships, including professional connections. This is someone who felt, and possibly was, overlooked and underappreciated during her formative years."

"That's the consensus—about her contentiousness, I mean."

"She would take pride in the fact that she did not 'negotiate.' It's probable her ego would get in the way of any successful negotiation. Her intense emotional investment in every point of conflict would leave her two paths: to shut down entirely, or to call upon a higher authority to mediate."

Jason said, "Resulting in all those filed complaints and trivial charges."

"Correct."

Jason thought it over. "She could have threatened the wrong person with legal action."

"This is not someone who would be good at reading the room," agreed the man who rarely acknowledged there was a room to be read.

So, not anything Jason didn't already know, though hearing Sam's impressions helped clarify his thoughts.

Anyone could be the victim of a violent crime. That was a fact. But one of the four concepts in the theory of victimology was that of Victim Precipitation, the idea that some people actually initiated the confrontation that eventually led to their injury or death. For example, some personalities might be so abrasive and obnoxious, they inadvertently triggered victimization.

This was not to say the victim was to blame, but it was sort of like a fatal traffic accident. The pedestrian might have the right of way, but walking into the path of a speeding vehicle was still going to get you killed—speaking as the guy who'd started the day narrowly missing being mowed down by a speeding vehicle.

"The old man's banging the housekeeper," J.J. informed Jason over shrimp tacos at El Cartel that evening.

Jason managed to swallow before he started coughing. When he could speak again, he asked hoarsely, "Which old man?"

"The former senator. Ono. He's banging the housekeeper. She's like thirty years younger than him."

J.J. Russell fit everyone's preconception of what an FBI agent should look like. He was tall, square-jawed, with dark hair that fell in a little wave so perfect, it could have been permed. He'd been top of his class at the Academy, but though he was smart, capable, and ambitious, he was not popular at the LA Field Office. He was just a little too cocky for someone who was barely out of probation. And he had an unfortunate tendency to blame—and then backbite—his partner when things went wrong.

A painful run-in with BAU Chief Sam Kennedy, and getting partnered with Kennedy's boyfriend—a rising star in the ACT—had curbed the latter tendency, though he was still pretty cocky.

To their mutual surprise, Jason and J.J. actually made an okay team. After Montana, they were even *almost* friends. Or at least friendly.

"He's a widower, right?" Jason asked.

"Right."

"Well, then. Consenting adults."

"The family's afraid he's going to leave everything to her."

"If it's his to leave, then..." Jason shrugged. "When you say *family*, who's included in that?"

"The senator's surviving sister still lives in the house with him and the housekeeper. She's been a goldmine of information. The sister. Not the housekeeper."

"I bet."

"Cynical, West. And sexist." J.J. was grinning.

"Maybe," Jason acknowledged. "What about Georgette's siblings?"

"Two brothers and a sister. She wasn't close to any of them." J.J. scowled as the filling fell out of the bottom of his taco.

"There aren't a lot of family photos in her apartment. She did have four pictures of a black-and-white cat."

"The cat now lives with the sister. Françoise."

"Is Françoise the cat or the sister?"

"The sister. The cat's name is Hammett."

"Ah."

"Anyway, Ono's parents are deceased. Her father when she was seventeen. Her mother three years ago. The remaining family consists of her siblings, her great-aunt, and her grandfather. Only the grandfather believes further investigation into her death is required."

"The brothers and sister believe her death was accidental?"

"Yep. And given the circumstances, you can understand why they feel like the less attention, the better."

Jason frowned. "They're so concerned with how her death *looked*, they don't care whether she was actually murdered?"

"That's not what I said." J.J. thought it over. "Although, maybe. But you have to admit, the way she died is not good press."

Jason opened his mouth, and J.J. said, "Some kid turned her into a meme. It was floating around the campus intranet until the administration finally got it taken down. Not before the family saw it."

"Jesus."

"She was not popular."

"Even so." Poor Ono. He hoped she'd never read her Rate My Professor reviews.

J.J. shrugged. "Anyway, the only one pushing for the case to be reopened is the old man, and the rest of them believe that's because he feels guilty. He and Georgette had a blowup shortly before her death over his relationship with Ms. Suzuki."

"Suzuki is the housekeeper."

"Yep."

Jason thought it over. "Would there be financial incentive to get rid of Georgette?"

"I guess so. One less slice of the pie to divvy up when the old man goes. But those people are not hurting for money. They've all got trusts and healthy savings and retirement accounts. It's not like anyone hated her. They mostly seemed to view her as a nuisance."

"Nice."

"You don't get to pick your family. I bet Georgette would have voted them off the island too."

That was probably true.

"What about the Touchstone angle?"

J.J. grimaced, forking up the spilled cabbage and shrimp. "I don't know. It's falling apart, to be frank."

"Seriously?"

"Yeah."

Unexpected and disappointing. Jason pushed his dish away. "Were you able to find out who the officer was that Ono charged with sexual harassment?"

"Hugo Quintana. There's no paper on him. He worked as a guard at CIW Chino. They'd hire him back in a heartbeat."

"Did anyone bother checking into Ono's claim that she was being harassed?"

"Rice, the head of security, says he interviewed Quintana and was satisfied with his answers. He says Quintana is one of his best men. Happily married, with two daughters headed for college."

"Did you interview Quintana?"

"No. Do you want me to?"

Here's where J.J. was still a first office agent. "It couldn't hurt."

"True. But there's no evidence to support Ono's claim of harassment." J.J. met Jason's gaze and groaned. "I *know*. I'll talk to Quintana. It looked promising, but I don't think that line of inquiry is going anywhere."

Working as a guard at a women's correctional facility might have made Quintana a little less refined in his dealings with the, er, fairer sex. And Ono? Jason's inclination was always to side with his victim, but he couldn't argue that Ono's extensive history of complaints and grievances weakened her credibility.

"What about Eli Humphrey?" J.J. asked. "You haven't interviewed him yet, have you?"

"He's out of town until Friday."

J.J.'s nod was noncommittal.

"What?" Jason said. "You think I'm grabbing for straws?"

"I think you don't like striking out."

"Nobody likes striking out. That's not what this is about. I'm not personally invested here. It's just…"

"Aren't you? You think Ono was murdered."

"I do. Yes."

"But there's nothing evidentiary to support that. It's a hunch. Meanwhile, we've got cases piling up. *You've* got cases piling up." He studied Jason and said knowingly, "Speaking of being out of town, Shane Donovan says there's intel that Shepherd Durrand might be planning to return to the States."

It was like someone flipped a switch—that flash of excitement, that flare of *I knew it.*

"Donovan told you that when?"

"This afternoon."

It was almost physical, that desire—*need*—to hurry up and close the book on Ono, get this done and dusted so he could take another whack at Fletcher-Durrand, the one that got away, the case that mattered—

Except. This case mattered too. Ono mattered too. He was not closing the book on her until he was confident she had not met with foul play. Too bad if she had been difficult or unlikeable or had even precipitated her own demise. Too bad if it was embarrassing to the family or irritating to her colleagues or frustrating for himself and Russell. This was the job. This was the assignment.

He said mildly, "Then like they say in the movies, we better *go, go, go.* I need to be able to look Senator Ono in the eyes when I tell him his granddaughter wasn't murdered. Which means I need to believe it myself."

CHAPTER THIRTEEN

"**S**nowball in Hell," Jason taste-tested the title. Pretty apropos given the hours he'd spent scouring Georgie Ono's library for books on film noir.

After he'd left J.J., Jason had headed back to Touchstone and Ono's home office. His conversation with his partner had reminded him of a key facet of Ono's character. She was a collector. Per her grandfather and Detective Child, she had put herself into financial jeopardy buying rare and out-of-print films. Which, Jason deduced, meant she had put together a significant collection: significant enough for her former boyfriend to attempt to lay claim to it, and for her family to formally donate it to UCLA's archive. You didn't formally donate a dozen DVDs and a VHS copy of *The Maltese Falcon*.

If there was one personality type Jason knew as well as Sam knew his psychos and socios, it was the fanatical collector.

Until now, he hadn't taken too seriously Grandpa Ono's insistence that a lost noir film might provide motive for Georgie's death. But Calida Lois's bitter comment about Georgie caring more about losing an imaginary film than a real-life relationship resonated.

It wasn't so much about *what* people collected as it was the psychology of collecting. Something like forty percent of the population collected various things—everything from china thimbles to Old Masters. As to *why* humans collected the things they did, theories abounded. From the effort to impose order on a chaotic world to attempting to build financial wealth and/or social status, there was plenty of conjecture regarding collecting and collectors.

Frequently, the collectors Jason had encountered viewed collecting as embarking on a great quest. The hunt was a big part of the attraction, but so was possessing something no one else could have. Even so, it was during that initial stage of craving the desired object—the as-yet-unfilled art collector's imaginings as to what rewards this particular golden fleece would bring—that delight of acquisition burned the brightest. *Anticipating* possession seemed to be even more pleasurable than having possession.

Georgie, from everything Jason could discover, had still been in that fever haze of longing for something just out of reach. Something tantalizingly close but not yet possessed. Lois believed that the deal, whatever it was, had fallen through.

But one thing Jason knew about collectors: they did not give up easily.

They did not always take no for an answer.

Georgie did not seem like someone who would take no for an answer.

So Jason had started his own hunt, and he thought maybe he'd found what Georgie had been after.

She'd sure been fond of her sticky notes and highlighters, but eventually he'd figured out her system. Or at least he'd worked out that the lavender adhesives were all stuck to pages with references, even if only the most fleeting, to an obscure 1957 film noir titled *Snowball in Hell.*

The film had starred two largely unknown (at least to Jason) actors. David Aubrey had played crime reporter Nathan Doyle, and Joe North had portrayed police lieutenant Matthew Spain.

A description of the film read: *It's 1943, and the world is at war. Reporter Nathan Doyle, newly returned from the European Theater, is asked to cover the murder of a society blackmailer—a man who, Homicide Detective Matthew Spain believes, Doyle had every reason to want dead.*

Okay. A classic film noir setup, though noir was reaching the end of its heyday in 1957.

The film was supposedly based on "real-life characters" (a misnomer if there ever was one) and was the last to be directed by Henry Walsh, who'd had a nice little string of noirish successes before falling victim to the Hollywood Blacklist.

With a blacklisted director and a reportedly homoerotic subtext, it was no wonder the film had quickly and quietly sunk into oblivion, only ever showing in a handful of art-film theaters. By the mid-'60 *Snowball in Hell* had achieved cult status but was only available in chopped-up prints that had been severely edited for late night TV. By 1978, the film was officially classified as "incomplete or partially lost."

Current status: *a few fragments and a trailer survive at the UCLA Film and Television Archive. Also, a six-minute reel was found in the Portuguese Archive, which was copied to safety stock.*

At one time, the soundtrack was believed to exist, but that seemed to have also disappeared. Maybe not surprising, given that the statistics for film in general—and the silents in particular—were pretty grim.

According to a study by the Library of Congress, seventy-five percent of all silent films were believed lost. Whether the numbers were quite that catastrophic, there was no doubt a huge amount of work was gone forever.

The survival odds for films made after the '50s were higher, but still not great. There were all too many reasons for old films to go missing, including the common use of nitrate film. Not only did nitrate film deteriorate easily, it was *highly* flammable, and the resulting fires virtually unextinguishable. Unsurprisingly, that terrible combination had resulted in several disastrous studio fires, including a famously destructive one in the MGM vault.

But nitrate wasn't the only reason so many films had been lost over time. Almost unbelievable shortsightedness and lack of imagination had also played a part. Black-and-white film prints had commonly been incinerated to salvage the silver image particles in their emulsions. Films disappeared when production companies went bankrupt. Sometimes, bafflingly, studios remade films and destroyed the original to eliminate comparisons or competition, or cannibalized set pieces that were then repurposed for new productions. Sometimes old films were simply junked to provide storage space for new films.

Film archivists were working against the clock in a way other art preservationists were not.

Jason could see why Georgie had bought into the possibility that *Snowball in Hell* still existed. For one thing, there was no apocryphal story of its destruction in a particular vault or at a particular studio. For another, bits and pieces of it *did* exist.

But *how* had she learned the film still possibly existed? How would that have come to her attention?

Who had contacted her? And why *her*?

If the film really did exist, why wouldn't the possessor of the print go to one of the large and reputable archives? In particular, why not approach UCLA's archive?

Especially puzzling, given the competing budgets of an institution like UCLA versus Georgette Ono's strained credit cards.

Maybe there *was* something suspish in the film's provenance.

Or…

What if Georgie had done the approaching?

But, again, how would Georgie become aware of the film's existence?

Jason bit his thumbnail, thinking. He remembered his conversation with Alex. They'd been talking about cams and bootlegs and their role in film preservation. They'd been talking about YouTube.

"'Broadcast Yourself,'" Jason quoted, turning his laptop on.

It was long after midnight when Jason finally clicked on the "Boogie Man" channel and watched, bleary-eyed, as the clip began to play.

"Lt. Matthew Spain" was seated alone in his office when reporter "Nathan Doyle" was shown in. The detective nodded to Doyle's police escort, who backed out, shutting the door.

Jason paused the YouTube video, studying the two men frozen forever on the black-and-white screen. Both the picture and sound of this four-minute snippet of *Snowball in Hell* was remarkably good quality. The costume and set design weren't bad either. And the two leads, Joe North playing Matthew Spain and David Aubrey playing Nathan Doyle were both startlingly handsome, though in very different ways.

Jason jotted down a couple of notes, then pressed Play.

"Sit down," Spain said, and Doyle pulled out a chair and sat down on the other side of the tidy desk. Spain looked crisp and clean-shaven in a dark suit. He reached for a cup of coffee, and the camera focused briefly on the wedding band on his left hand.

A little cue, a little clue, for a particular audience. Jason made another quick note.

"Coffee?" Spain asked politely. "Smoke?"

"Thanks."

Spain poured him a cup of coffee from a flask. Doyle swallowed a mouthful. The camera followed Doyle's gaze to a photograph of a pretty, smiling, dark-haired woman on the bookshelf behind the desk. Next to the photograph was a long and probably pointed row of books on the law and police procedure.

Spain proffered a pack of cigarettes, Camels—did they do product placement in the 1950s?—Doyle took one, and Spain leaned forward to light it for him. Spain's hands were large and well-shaped. His lashes made dark crescents against his cheekbones. As though feeling Doyle's stare, Spain raised his eyes—and the two men locked gazes.

Probably one of the hottest romantic movie moments Jason had ever seen. Right there with Jennifer Tilly's seductive Violet when she eased down her bra strap to share her ink with Gina Gershon's Corky in *Bound*. Or André Holland's Kevin and Trevante Rhodes's Chiron gazing into each other's eyes as they listened to the song "Hello Stranger," in *Moonlight*.

Jason had to wonder if the two actors, North and Aubrey, had been having some secret off-screen affair or if they were just really, really good.

Chemistry wasn't always sexual. Or even romantic.

Doyle stared into Spain's long-lashed eyes, and his expression changed, the camera capturing the moment when Doyle realized Spain knew his secret. Knew exactly what he was. Doyle glanced at Spain's desktop as though somehow the explanation could be found there.

Even in black and white, Jason could almost see the blood rushing to Doyle's face, and just as quickly draining away. Doyle's eyelashes fluttered like he was about to keel over, but then he drew back, taking a long, studied draw on his cigarette. He sat very straight.

Spain flicked his lighter closed, put it away. He seemed to be in no hurry.

"Why am I here?" Doyle blew out a long stream of smoke. The use of cigarettes—everything from lighting them to smoking them—really was an art form in twentieth century cinema. Talk about coded messages.

Spain watched Doyle with burning intensity. "Why didn't you mention you were with the Arlen kid on Saturday night?"

"I wasn't with him," Doyle said. "I ran into him at the Las Palmas Club. We had a drink together." He shrugged.

"Were you with him when Claire Arlen and her brother showed up?"

Doyle hesitated. "Me and half the bar."

"What happened?"

Aubrey's voice was light and pleasant, but it wasn't the voice of a 1950s leading man. In the 1950s, leading men had deep, commanding voices. Aubrey was probably the better actor, but North had the tone and presence of a movie star. And yet North didn't seem to have achieved movie-star status either. Was that because of his sexuality? Or because out of all the hundreds and hundreds of working actors out there, almost none of them ever achieved movie-star status?

Doyle said, "Claire arrived with her brother, Carl, and asked Phil to come home. He declined. She got upset and said some things. She'd been drinking, I think. Anyway, Carl convinced her to leave. That's pretty much it."

Spain grinned, and on screen or off, that would have been a smile hard to resist. "Well, that's a very careful, factual recounting of what took place. I bet you're a pretty good reporter. You understand the power of words. Other people we've interviewed have used words like *screamed* and *threatened* and *demanded*."

"Like I said, she'd had a few drinks. Her brother took her home before she could get into any real trouble."

Spain leaned back in his swivel chair and rubbed his chin. "Listen, Sir Galahad, it might interest you to know that the lady in question didn't mind throwing you to the wolves. She said it looked to her like you were pretty angry with Philip yourself. Like you were mad enough to kill."

"She doesn't know me very well." Doyle studied the ashes on his cigarette.

"Did she threaten to kill her husband and Pearl Jarvis?"

"She might have." Doyle's smile was wry. Yes, Aubrey was definitely the stronger actor. He almost had a James Dean quality, although he seemed more fragile, less dynamic. "I wasn't listening that carefully, to tell you the truth."

"Why's that?"

Doyle said slowly, "I went there for a few drinks and some laughs, but after I got there…I realized that really wasn't what I needed."

"What did you need?" Spain asked, and in the pause that followed, Jason realized his heart was pounding in recognition of what a chance these two men were taking at that time and that place in history.

Well, that was the magic of film, wasn't it? It had the power to make you feel what you could never experience for yourself.

But it wasn't just the characters taking a risk. The two actors were taking a risk as well. Homosexuality in the 1950s was still classified as a mental illness as well as being widely prosecuted as criminal behavior. California had been more enlightened than a lot of states, but even in California, homosexuals were discriminated against and victimized. As for working for the FBI? As far as the Bureau was concerned—and J. Edgar Hoover aside—there was no gay in G-man. *Any* G-man.

That didn't mean people didn't find a way to fall in love and live their lives.

People always found a way.

Neither man on the screen spoke. Neither man looked away.

The door to the office opened, and a tall, gray-haired detective entered. "Loot, the Jarvis girl never—"

The film clip ended.

That was it. Four grainy minutes of what looked to be a well-made if depressing film. After all, in 1957 there were no happy endings for gay characters. One, if not both, of these guys would be dead by the time the final credits rolled.

Even so, he could see why Georgie Ono would have been eager to recover a complete copy of the film.

He found the email address for Boogie Man, checked the little I AM NOT A ROBOT captcha box, and apparently sent a message without any words in it. Which was maybe okay, since he wasn't sure what to ask anyway. *Where the hell did you find this clip?*

That would certainly be a starting point.

Also, probably, an ending point.

Boogie Man's channel was five years old. The library consisted of nine videos, three of which were partial films. The clip from *Snowball in Hell* was four years old, and it appeared to have been the last to be uploaded. Boogie Man had not been active for the last two years.

This could very well be a dead end, but it was still progress. Jason now knew which lost film Georgie had been after. He knew why she believed the film was out there somewhere, though he couldn't be sure that Boogie Man's YouTube channel was where she had discovered its existence.

He understood why, as a collector, she had been obsessed with finding the film. Just to view it in its entirety would have been a dream come true. To actually own it, to possess it? If a print of the full film did exist somewhere, then what Georgie had told her grandfather was probably true.

More than one of her fellow collectors might be willing to kill to get their hands on that print.

CHAPTER FOURTEEN

Jason was on the phone to SSA George Potts, his immediate supervisor at the LA Field Office, when he stepped out of the elevators and into the Archive Research and Study Center dungeon the next morning.

"I'm not pulling the plug," George was saying. "Even if I wanted to, I'd have to run it by Kapszukiewicz, though what the heck any of this has to do with Major Theft, I don't understand. But there's a lot going on right now. At the very least, I could really use Russell elsewhere."

"If you've got to pull Russell, I get it. And I'm used to working alone." Jason glanced to the left and started at the sight of Pop lurking in the shadows.

Okay, Pop wasn't lurking, he was hovering, waiting to intercept unauthorized visitors. Jason hastily juggled his phone and coffee cup, showing his ID like a vampire's prospective victim flashing a crucifix.

"Remember me?" he mouthed to Pop.

Pop clearly did remember because his scowling retreat was pure *Curses! Foiled again.*

"You still there?" George asked.

"Sorry. I missed that last bit."

"I know you're still responding to email and phone messages, but your case load is not getting any smaller. However, if you think your continued presence on site is necessary, then I guess that's that."

Jason protested, "It's only been three days, George." In theory, he had thirty days to conduct his assessment before he needed a supervisor's approval to extend the investigation.

"That's true, but you were gone for a week before this assignment started. Time which you're entitled to. *But.*"

All true. Both what George was saying and what he wasn't. Jason winced. He liked George. George was a good boss. He was fair and hardworking and tried to be supportive. He also tried diligently to avoid ever crossing swords with Washington, so if he was pressuring Jason to wrap things up, *he* had to be feeling the heat.

"No, you're right, George. This probably isn't the greatest allocation of resources."

"No, it's not. We're seriously shorthanded, buddy. That's all I'm saying. If you feel like you've got to be there on campus to carry out this investigation, okay. I'll say no more."

"If you can just give me until Friday? Then I'll know where I'm at." Conscious of Pop's suspicious hovering, Jason tried to keep his answers vague. Hopefully, Pop thought Jason was being chased by bill collectors.

"Absolutely." He could hear the relief in George's voice. "I don't mean to pressure you. But there's *a lot* coming down the pike. If you haven't heard about it yet, you soon will."

That sounded a little ominous, but as Jason rounded the corner of the rabbit warren of narrow halls and doorways, he spotted Alex waiting by his office. Alex nodded in greeting. He was not smiling.

Jason said hastily, "Right. I'll talk to you Friday. Thanks for calling." He disconnected and smiled hello. Alex continued to look uncharacteristically somber. "Morning. This is a surprise."

"Good morning."

"Everything okay?"

"Can we talk for a sec?"

"Of course."

Jason unlocked his office, stepped inside, and switched on the light. He dropped his keys and messenger bag on the desktop. "It's going to be another triple-digits day. It's already hot out there. Have a seat."

Alex hesitated. He glanced down the hall and then closed the door, which Jason read as Pop's reputation preceding him.

"Yeah, I don't think Pop cares much for me." Jason leaned against his desk, took a swallow of his coffee, trying to read Alex's expression.

Alex grimaced. "That's just Pop. He thinks the safety and security of the archive is all on him."

"Except the archive isn't here anymore."

Alex shrugged. "Old habits." He continued to consider Jason, as though trying to come to a decision.

"Maybe you should just say what's on your mind," Jason suggested.

Alex sighed, took a seat in front of the desk, and said, "I've been thinking over what we talked about Monday."

"Okay," Jason said cautiously. He thought he knew what was coming, so maybe George's phone call was timely.

"I..." He finally met Jason's gaze squarely. "I wasn't one hundred percent honest with you."

"I see."

"I mean, I like you, you know that, but the FBI thing is no bueno."

"I'm sorry you feel that way."

"I only mean, confiding in you is like confiding in the federal government, and that doesn't always turn out so well."

Jason couldn't help a mild, "In fairness, confiding in me isn't *always* like confiding in the federal government."

Alex gave a short laugh. "Yeah, well. But here's the thing. I don't know if anyone really believes Georgie killed herself, either by accident or on purpose. I feel like...people just don't care either way. Everybody's busy, everybody's got their own problems, and she was..."

"Difficult?" Jason supplied a little wearily.

"Yes. She was. The thing with Eli? She burned *a lot* of bridges."

"I keep hearing that."

"It wasn't just Georgie who lost friends. It started a whole wave of paranoia. People started worrying whether Uncle Sam was coming for their collections. Again."

Jason sighed. "Listen, I'm not here for anyone's film collection. The focus of my assignment is very narrow. I want to reassure Professor Ono's family that there was no foul play in her death."

"But you can't," Alex said.

"No," Jason admitted. "As of right now, I can't. It's not like I have suspects or motives or anything. Just a gut feeling."

Alex nodded, gazed at the blank wall behind Jason as though looking for the answers there. Jason waited silently, patiently, for Alex to come to his decision. The way his morning was going, he was not feeling optimistic.

"I don't—can't—believe anybody killed Georgie. But if someone did, if I'm wrong…I'm not on that person's side. Especially someone who could do something so cruel and humiliating."

"It was crueler than it had to be." That bothered Jason too.

Finally, Alex said, "I don't think anyone would—but if it did happen, it was probably one of the guys in our film club."

Jason didn't blink, didn't bat an eye. Here was the confirmation he'd been looking for. The cinephile supper club Senator Ono had spoken of was real. The fallout from Georgie going to the police about Eli Humphrey might indeed have played a role in her death.

Also, troublingly, Alex was a lot more involved in Jason's case than Jason had hoped.

"Who else belongs to this film club?"

Alex made a face, shook his head. "People come and go. I'm really not comfortable naming names. What I *am* willing to do is bring you to our next screening as my guest. As my date, I guess. Anything after that introduction is up to you. But I'm warning you, if you do go after these people for copyright infringement or piracy or any of that bullshit…"

Alex didn't complete his thought because what was there to threaten Jason with? *I won't like you? We won't be friends anymore?* They weren't friends now. Friendly, yes.

Jason dismissed that cynical thought. The truth was, he did like Alex, and he did appreciate his cooperation. He'd do his best not to betray Alex's trust. He was sincere about the narrow scope of his investigation—he wasn't forgetting the lesson of Montana. And frankly, the more he learned about film preservation, the more ambivalent his feelings were about the Bureau's lack of a nuanced approach to some pretty complicated issues.

"I appreciate the offer, and I promise you I'm looking for a murderer—who may or may not exist. I'll do my best not to jeopardize your standing within that community."

Alex nodded, unconvinced. "Truthfully, I didn't want to do this, but murder trumps social awkwardness."

"I'm glad you think so. When's the next film screening?"

"Friday. We're meeting at Eli Humphrey's home in Beverly Hills. Supper's at eight. We usually have cocktails about seven thirty."

"It turns out my social calendar is empty."

"Great." Alex looked less than thrilled. "Where should I pick you up?"

Jason considered and rejected all scenarios that might result in future complications. "Here. I'll leave my car in the faculty parking. You can drop me off afterward."

"That'll work." Alex rose. He looked preoccupied and a little grim.

Jason rose too. "Listen, Alex, chances are, we have a nice meal, watch an interesting movie, and that's that."

Alex nodded, but what he said was, "I wish I believed that. The truth is, there's something off."

"Off?"

"Something's not right about those guys. I don't know what. I can't put my finger on it. But something's been off for a while." His smile was sour. "Maybe you'll figure it out before they figure you out."

After the office door closed behind Alex, Jason tried giving Sam a call.

He'd dozed off twice during their conversation the previous evening, and Sam had finally, wryly, told him to go to sleep and they'd talk tonight.

His call went straight to message. That wasn't unusual, of course. Sam was a busy guy. What was unusual was that Jason didn't get a return phone call before he had to leave for his first class of the day. Even then, it wasn't so out of the ordinary as to trigger concern. Sam was well aware that he and Jason didn't share the same sleep patterns, so it wasn't like he was going to take offense at Jason nodding off in the middle of a recounting of Sam's day.

Not that Sam really recounted his day in any but the most general terms.

Sam spent a lot of time in meetings—his least favorite thing about the job—so that was the most likely explanation for his lack of response.

It *was* a little surprising when Jason still hadn't heard back after the ninety-minute Celluloid Closet seminar concluded. Even if Sam didn't have time to talk, he'd typically leave a message to that effect.

Jason tried phoning again, and once again, his call went straight to message.

"Touching base," he said and clicked off.

If there was an actual reason to be worried about Sam, he'd already know. Jonnie or someone else would already have been in touch. So, Sam was just...offline.

It was puzzling but still not alarming. Even after their recent rough patch—or maybe because of it—Jason knew that if Sam was, inexplicably, angry with him, he wouldn't ghost him. In fact, it would be the opposite. Sam would be up in Jason's face—or at least his FaceTime—spelling out his displeasure in terms there was no mistaking.

Simmer down, West.

It's not like he'd said it was urgent he hear from Sam. If Sam was busy, he'd figure whatever it was could wait till that evening. Which was perfectly true.

After the conversation with George that morning, it was clear he couldn't afford to waste time. He used the time before his next class to search YouTube for more bits and pieces of *Snowball in Hell*.

Eventually he came across several uploads of the movie's official trailer.

Dramatic music, opening shot of oil derricks nodding knowingly against the ominous sky—foreshadowing *Chinatown*'s opening?—and...a soggy corpse being dragged out of La Brea tar pits.

"Hell of a thing," said the tall, gray-haired detective of the snippet Jason had watched the night before.

"Hell of a thing," Matthew Spain agreed.

The camera panned to a group of reporters smoking and talking beside snarling cement saber-toothed tigers, zoomed in on Nathan Doyle lighting a cigarette for a female reporter. Doyle looked across at Spain, the camera lingered.

"Yeah, it was a hell of a thing," Joe North said in the voice over. *"A society kidnapping gone about as wrong as a thing could go."*

More overwrought music and melting retro movie font spelling out: BLACKMAIL…BETRAYAL…MURDER!

(So much for alliteration.)

There were frames introducing the two main characters, looking good in fedoras as each spoke a line of cryptic dialog, and then a few seconds of what looked like the two main characters in a shootout with each other.

"I knew it," muttered Jason.

And, finally, there was the usual *Coming Soon to a Theater Near You!* and studio info.

Jason replayed the trailer a couple of times, thinking things over.

The actors playing Spain and Doyle looked to be in their late twenties-early thirties, so they'd be getting up there, but might still be around. Jason could probably determine that much from their IMDb filmographies, assuming they'd made more than one film.

He let his fingers do the walking down the mean streets of the internet and learned that David Aubrey had made three films after *Snowball in Hell*. They were all standard B fare monster movies, where he was inevitably cast as a bewildered-looking love interest for a buxom beauty being menaced by apes or aliens. He'd died of a drug overdose in 1967 at age 37.

It seemed unlikely any unauthorized film prints had come out of that quarter.

Joe North, on the other hand, had married three times and had a long list of film and TV credits, which just went to prove how little time Jason spent at the movies. North's last TV appearance had been in 1990. Jason couldn't find an obituary, so it was possible North was still out there somewhere. Which meant it was possible North was the source of this alleged print of *Snowball in Hell*.

There were other possibilities, including everyone in the cast and crew of *Snowball in Hell*. There were also plenty of other ways a film could fall into unauthorized hands.

While *Snowball in Hell* did not appear to have been widely distributed, release prints had been made and provided to theaters. Projectionists were often a source of pirated films. But hell, random citizens were known to discover lost works, like the eBay buyer who'd purchased a can of nitrate film and discovered Chaplin's *Zepped*. Or the lost 1962 Chinese film *Big and Little Wong Tin Bar*, which had been found on YouTube in 2016. So.

Was it *likely* a complete print of *Snowball in Hell* was floating out there on eBay or YouTube or in somebody's great-uncle's attic? No. But it *was* possible. Georgie Ono was a naturally suspicious person. If she'd been trying to get the money together to purchase the print, she had to have seen something that convinced her the film existed. Something more than the bits and pieces Jason had so far uncovered.

Had Georgie's interest in *Snowball in Hell* predated being approached by a seller? Or had the opportunity of purchasing the film sparked her obsession? The question was important because if her hunt for the film predated being approached by a possible seller—if her interest was widely known in the cinephile community—it was possible she had been the target of a well-thought-out scam.

Which might explain why the "seller"—after getting to know Georgie a bit better—had reconsidered making her his next victim.

But if the film did exist, if the attempt to sell had been sincere (even if there had been second thoughts), then there was a more than decent chance the print had come from a private collection or the estate of someone involved in the film's production.

Since his hunt had to begin somewhere, tracking down the cast and crew was as good a place to start as any.

It was nearly five when Jason returned from showing *The Birds* to students in the Hitchcock and His Influence class. Halfway through the film, he'd realized Dahle's notes were actually for an older Hitchcock film called *Blackmail*, so he'd had to resort to bluffing his way through the thirty minutes of discussion that followed. He could only imagine his next batch of Rate My Professor's Substitute scores.

To add to his chagrin, Sam had still not returned his phone calls.

This time Jason called Jonnie despite the fact that it was nearly eight on the East Coast and he'd probably be disturbing her at home.

The phone rang a couple of times, and then Jonnie answered with, "Hey. I was trying to decide whether to call you. Have you heard from Sam?"

Chapter Fifteen

Jason's heart stopped, and yet he heard himself say very calmly, "What does that mean? Isn't he there?"

"He flew to Wyoming first thing this morning. He's not answering his phone."

"Wyoming? Why? Did something happen to his mother?"

Jason had met Ruby Kennedy back in April when they'd stayed at her farm while he'd been on sick leave. Mrs. Kennedy appeared to be a hale and hearty sixtysomething, but you never knew.

"As far as I can tell, his mother's fine. I'm pretty sure this has to do with the Roadside Ripper case. He said he wanted to hike up to a place called Vedauwoo."

"Hike? Vedauwoo?"

Vedauwoo Recreation Area, a picturesque rock formation on Pole Mountain, was a popular destination for rock climbers, hikers, and mountain bikers. None of which described Sam.

It was also popular with artists.

In his mind's eye, Jason saw again a painting of sentinel pine trees, stark outcrops, and mournful moonlight. Ethan's painting. Vedauwoo had been one of Ethan's favorite spots to work.

"Why?"

"No clue. He got an idea into his head. You know how he is."

"I know he doesn't turn off his phone for hours."

"No. But…" Jonnie sounded troubled.

"But what?"

"I'm not sure," she admitted. "Something's up with him. He's been different ever since we found out about the existence of Bone Road."

"But it wasn't his case. He wasn't BAU Chief back then." Jason wasn't sure who he was trying to convince, since Jonnie already knew everything he was and wasn't saying, and Sam… wasn't listening.

Besides, Sam believed Ethan had fallen victim to the Roadside Ripper, so this wasn't a usual case, and Sam's usual ruthless logic was liable to be MIA.

"I know."

"What the hell could he be looking for?"

"I don't know."

"Why would he go alone? He's smarter than that."

She said patiently, "I'm not sure that he *is* alone. He didn't offer any details beyond where he was headed. It's not that I'm worried, exactly, but I thought I'd hear from him by now."

Jason said tersely, "*I'm* worried."

"Sorry about that. I just figured if anyone knew what was going on, it would be you."

"I know some people at the Cheyenne RA. I'll touch base with them and phone you back."

"Okay. Thanks, Jason. I appreciate it. He can be a real SOB, but he kind of grows on you after a while."

Jason muttered, "Tell me about it," and hung up. It took a minute or two to locate the personal phone number for Charles Reynolds, SAC of the Cheyenne Resident Agency, and one of Sam's oldest friends.

This time he didn't worry about the late hour or disturbing someone at home. He pressed the number and waited, impatiently counting the rings, until the phone picked up and a familiar, raspy male voice said, "Reynolds residence."

So FBI.

"Hey, Chuck. Sorry to call this late. This is Jason West, Sam's—"

"He *just* walked in the door," Reynolds interrupted. "You can go first, then I'll take my turn."

A couple of heartbeats of silence followed as the phone was handed over, and Jason's massive relief gave way to equally massive exasperation.

"He—"

"What the hell, Sam!"

"Sorry?" For once in his life Sam sounded nonplussed.

"I've been calling you all fucking *day*. Where the hell were you? Jonnie's scared to death. Why the hell wouldn't you let me know—tell *someone* where you were going? What the hell are you doing out there on your own?"

Jason was forced to stop for breath, and Sam said, as though for the nth time, "There's no cell reception once you're past Forest Road 700." So that was probably directed at Reynolds as well as Jason. "Of course I would have phoned you back. I'm sorry you were worried." Which was likely true and the correct thing to say, but delivered in a weary, strained-patience sort of voice that did little to soothe Jason's acerbated nerves. "I *told* Jonnie I was taking a personal day and where I'd be."

"A p-p-personal day?" Jason stuttered as though the concept was foreign, and frankly it *was* foreign in connection with Sam Kennedy. Not counting their stay in Wyoming, Sam had never taken time off for so much as a dental appointment, as far as Jason could tell. "You flew to *Wyoming* for a personal day? Why wouldn't you tell me this last night?"

Sam said with grim humor, "Are you sure I didn't?"

Jason was not amused. "I'd remember that." Was Sam really not going to say where he'd been and what he'd been up to? Did he imagine Jonnie would not have mentioned Vedauwoo? Or that Jason wouldn't understand the significance of that place?

Not that Jason was one hundred percent sure he understood the significance in this context. But he understood that something was going on with Sam.

"Listen. West." Sam stopped, sighed. He said, choosing his words, "I didn't realize I'd be out of range for so long. It took longer to hike back to my car than I thought. That's all. I promise you we'll talk tomorrow. Okay?"

Tomorrow? No. Not okay.

Except it would have to be okay because Sam was standing in Chuck Reynolds's kitchen, waiting to talk to Chuck next, and besides, he'd already apologized and promised to explain further, so to continue this would simply be Jason venting his feelings, including his worry that there was something to *really* worry about.

He clipped out, "Yep. Okay."

Sam seemed to hesitate, then repeated, "I'll talk to you tomorrow," and disconnected.

Jesus. He'd devoted all of forty-five seconds to reassure and comfort Jason.

Okay, despite the brief scare, Jason didn't need reassurance or comfort. It would have been nice to hear one of those taciturn *I love yous*, but Sam's PDAs were few and far between, and clearly he had more important things on his mind.

Jason stewed for a minute or two, then called Jonnie, who confirmed that Sam had mentioned taking a personal day, but that she'd put as little credence in it as Jason because, like Jason, she viewed Sam and personal days as likely a combo as oil and water.

"Even on his personal days, he's calling in every couple of hours," she pointed out.

"I know. I agree."

"I didn't realize this place was so remote."

Jason answered vaguely. Another unpleasant thought had occurred to him.

Even if Sam had been out of cell phone range while hiking in the National Park, he had to have seen all those messages after he got back to his vehicle. Why hadn't he responded then? Why had he waited until after driving all the way back to Laramie? Until Jason phoned him?

Balthasar Bardolf—BB to his friends—looked like a dashing undertaker in a steampunk video game. He was a willowy six-foot-four and wore a purple silk jacquard waistcoat and moto boots. His hair was red and swooped back from his long, narrow face. His eyes were blue. He didn't wear a top hat, which was a missed opportunity, in Jason's opinion, but he carried a pocket watch, which he used to good effect in brushing off Jason when he tried to introduce himself Thursday morning.

"Sorry, I have to be someplace," Bardolf told him. "But welcome to the asylum."

"Thanks," Jason replied to Bardolf's retreating back. "Later." He meant it.

However, *later* did not materialize.

Although in theory, Professor Bardolf was on the UCLA campus that day, he might as well have been in Santa Clarita or perhaps his moving fortress. When the man was not in class, he was in his office meeting with students or on the phone. If Jason hadn't known better, he'd have thought Bardolf was avoiding him, but no way had Bern tipped off the archivist as to Jason's real job description, so unless Alex was the tipster (which, at this point, seemed equally unlikely), it was just irksome coincidence.

While Jason considered Bardolf a person of interest in his investigation, he was only one of several leads yet to be followed up, so with a class-free day before him, Jason returned his attention to hunting down the remaining cast and crew members of *Snowball in Hell*.

It was a time-consuming process, but that was something he was used to.

A lot—maybe the majority—of his investigations were largely conducted online or over the phone.

He started with Director Henry Walsh.

Walsh had died in France in 1981.

Producer Leeland Wheeler had died in Hollywood in 1975.

Director of Photography Dudley Saunders had died in Granada Hills in 1980, and so it went. Art Director, Film Editor, Assistant Director, Sound, Special Effects, Visual Effects, Camera and Electrical, and on and on and on.

Jason scratched a quick, tidy line through one name after another.

The End.

How had he never noticed how many people were involved in making movies? Even a little indie project involved a staggering number of people working behind the scenes.

Not all these people would have access to the film pre-production, during production, or post-production, but enough would have had access at various stages to make his task a daunting one. More daunting once he realized pretty much his entire cast of suspects had moved on to that great screening room in the sky.

With the exception of Yolanda Flowers, who had played reporter Tara Renee, and Joe North, who had played Lieutenant Matthew Spain, everyone involved in *Snowball in Hell* was out of Jason's reach.

For all he knew, Yolanda and Joe were also out of his reach, but they were not listed as deceased on IMDb, and subsequent searching turned up nothing.

In Yolanda's case, the missing obit was probably an oversight. She had mostly played bit parts. In fact, the character of Tara Renee had been her largest role. Her filmography ended with an uncredited appearance as a Mrs. Twickenham in *The F.B.I.* TV series in 1967.

But Joe North…

Joe North had had a long if not illustrious career, and the more Jason searched movie databases, the more convinced he was North must still be alive.

Not working, obviously. He'd be in his nineties.

He could be tracked through his Medicare and social security. In fact, even if he wasn't working, he'd still be getting residuals or royalties or something like that, right?

All that television work in the '60s and '70s meant North had to have been a member of SAG—now SAG-AFTRA. The Screen Actors Guild - American Federation of Television and Radio Artists was the labor union for television actors, journalists, radio personalities, recording artists, singers, voice actors, and, these days, internet influencers, fashion models, and other media professionals.

SAG-AFTRA's Professional Representatives Department franchised talent agents worldwide, which meant there was a strong likelihood North's agent had also been a union member. The national headquarters was located on Wilshire Blvd. in Los Angeles, but a patient fifty-five minutes on the phone got Jason the information he needed.

Though Herman Alban—North's agent—was deceased, the Alban Agency was still around, and thirty minutes after contacting them, Jason had the address and phone number of Joseph Edward Gant's (North was Joe's stage name).

Promisingly, North—rather, Gant—lived in North Hollywood.

Jason phoned the number and mentally crossed his fingers.

He was expecting a phone machine, but a woman's voice, a deep, pleasant contralto, answered.

Jason introduced himself, gave the abbreviated version of what he was after, and Mary Beth Eristoff, "one of Joe's roommates," handed him off to "Joey."

"FBI, heh?" The voice that came on the line was higher and thinner than expected, but by then Jason had sat through enough video clips of Joe North to recognize it. "You're too late. The statute of limitations has run out."

"Statute of limitations on what?" Jason asked.

He realized that funny croaking sound was Joe North laughing. "You name it, pal. I've done it all."

"That sounds promising," Jason said, and Joe North started croaking again.

The croaking cut off abruptly to be replaced with hissing sounds. It took Jason a second to recognize several people were whispering.

"Hello?"

Joe North returned to the conversation. "You want an interview. Is that what I hear?"

Very rarely were subjects of his investigations quite this eager to talk, but Jason wasn't about to miss an opportunity. "I do. If it's convenient this after—"

North interrupted, "Why don't you come over now. The girls'll fix you lunch. Lulubelle wants to ask you a few questions."

Girls? Lunch? Lulubelle?

"Uhhhh, okay," Jason said doubtfully.

"Don't worry," cackled North. "They don't bite. *Too* much!"

The house was on Ben Avenue in North Hollywood. A 1929 Spanish-style charmer set back behind a desert cottage garden in riotous summer bloom. A little slice of Old Hollywood. All that was missing was a nubile starlet with a flower basket and two Scottie dogs.

Jason walked through the wrought-iron gate, followed the stone walk through the giant cactus and lavender bushes, up the steps to the double-wide front door.

A tall, thin woman with stick-straight silver hair and piercing blue eyes in a deeply tanned face answered the doorbell. She wore high-waisted men's trousers and a man's plaid shirt with the sleeves rolled up, and she was rocking that old-school lesbian vibe.

"You don't look like an FBI agent." The woman, who identified herself as *Margot*, seemed disappointed.

Jason offered his credentials' case. "I'm undercover as a Fuller Brush Man."

Margot laughed and waved away his identification. "You're too young to know what that is. You must watch a lot of movies."

"More than I used to," he admitted, putting his wallet away.

She led the way into a bright and airy white living room with glossy wooden floors and lots of windows looking onto the pretty garden. Despite the extensive—and no doubt expensive—renovations, the house still retained that vintage Hollywood charm. Or maybe the vintage Hollywood charm was coming from the room's inhabitants. An elderly man and two ladies of a certain age were seated on the comfortable, "modern cottage" furniture.

Jason didn't recognize the women, but the man was a crinkled-parchment version of Joe North.

North rose—still tall and straight-shouldered—and Jason shook hands. "Thanks for seeing me, Mr. North."

A tiny, elegant African American lady of about seventy, said, "You should have arrested him years ago. I would have thought *Heavy Evil* was sufficient grounds."

They all laughed, and Jason knew it was going to be a very long afternoon.

In fact, it was one of the easiest interviews of his career.

Typically, he wasn't fed lunch, let alone information, on china plates or in crystal glasses. But Joe North and company loved to eat, loved to drink, loved to talk, and *loved* visitors, even those carrying badges.

Granted, not everyone who had something to hide *realized* they had something to hide. Just look at Don Miller. That would be Don Miller the amateur archaeologist, not Don Miller the serial killer. Presumably, Don the serial killer had known he had something to hide. Over the course of his lifetime, Don the amateur archaeologist had amassed a treasure trove of thousands of artifacts, some legally, some illegally purchased. All were summarily confiscated by the government, which would probably spend the next fifty years trying to sort out which was which.

"That limey movie gets all the credit, but we were actually the first to use the word *homosexual* in an English-language film," North said over the chicken à la king. "That's to say, the word was on a book my character finds in the Doyle character's apartment." He took a sip of white wine, nodded to Margot, the silver-haired woman who had answered the door, and said, "Nice bouquet on this chardonnay. There's a subtle citrus undernote."

"Lovely peach aroma," agreed Margot.

North must have been a better actor than Jason realized because the majority of his roles had been handsome tough guys who mostly thought with their fists and almost always got the girl—barring those rare occasions he had to send her up the river. The reality was this genial, chatty old gentleman.

"You were married when you filmed *Snowball in Hell*, weren't you?" Jason asked.

"He was *always* married," Mary Beth, the small African American lady, commented, and once again the others laughed in chorus.

"I didn't know I had a choice," North said. "We didn't, really. Not back then. Not if you wanted a *real* career. I warned David plenty of times. He was a much better actor than me, but he just couldn't play the game."

"He was born into the wrong century," Lulubelle said sadly.

Lulubelle was the youngest of the group. She looked to be in her late fifties-early sixties, a curvaceous, aging, blonde bombshell who, apparently, was an aspiring writer of thrillers. She had already interrogated Jason about firearms training, profiling terrorists, and crimes on the high seas. Though saddened to learn that most of his cases involved trying to recover objects of cultural value, she was still making the most of her chance to grill a real live FBI agent.

"Were you and David Aubrey close?" Jason asked North.

"Not really." North winked. "Not as close as we'd have been if his pasty-faced boyfriend hadn't been hanging around all the time."

Margot said, "The movie was supposed to be inspired by real events, wasn't it? There really was a Doyle at the *Tribune-Herald*?"

North snorted. "That's what they said. Of course, they said that about a lot of films back then. *Based on a true story!*" His tone was mocking. "Anyway, they wouldn't have used his real name. You'd have lawsuits up the yin-yang."

"True." Lulubelle spoke with the authority of all aspiring authors. "Nothing ruins a career faster than a defamation lawsuit."

"I'm glad the film's getting a second chance at life, though. I did some of my best work in that picture. Aubrey thought it was going to be his big breakthrough."

Jason cautioned, "I'm not sure how much of a revival the film's going to have if a complete print can't be found. You were my best hope."

North shook his head regretfully. "It wouldn't have occurred to me to try to get a print of any film I was in. It's not like they handed 'em out as souvenirs. What would I have done with it? It wasn't like it is now days. Back then, you didn't pop a tape in a VCR if you wanted to see one of your old movies. I'd have had to stay up past my bedtime and watch it on late-night TV between all the porno commercials, like everybody else." He gave that croaky-frog laugh. "Anyway, I can't stand to watch myself. Never could."

"Joey has one of the original movie posters framed in the family room," Lulubelle said.

"I'd love to see it," Jason replied.

Accordingly, they moved the party into the spacious family room, and Jason admired North's vintage movie poster collection.

"Most of the times the posters were better than the movies," North admitted. "I used to look at those posters and wish I could be in *that* movie."

The artwork for *Snowball in Hell* was especially nice. The vibrant red-and-black representational style looked like the work of Reynold Brown or, more likely, an imitator.

The tag line across the bottom read: *We all have our stories, Mr. Doyle. Don't we?*

North said suddenly, "You know who *did* have a print? Of the film, I mean. Aubrey. Of course, by the time he died, he might have sold it for another hypo full of dreams."

"David Aubrey had a complete print of *Snowball in Hell*?"

"He said he did. I don't know why he'd lie about it. I don't know what good that does you either. He died a long time ago."

"1967." A decade after the movie had been made. And yes, that was a long time to hang on to a tin of film nobody else wanted.

"What about the boyfriend?" Lulubelle, the would-be crime writer, put in, and it was a good question. "Were they still together when Aubrey died?"

"I don't know if there's room for a third party in a junkie's life," North said. "I will say, that kid was crazy about Aubrey. Never took his eyes off him all the time we were shooting."

"I wouldn't either with you on the scene," teased Mary Beth.

Jason couldn't quite get a fix on this household. The women all seemed to have worked for various studios at various times, so was that the connection? Were they all simply good pals and roommates? Nobody appeared to be a blood relation. Lulubelle and Mary Beth seemed like they might be a couple, but all four of them were extremely comfortable, even cozy. It was nice, but puzzling.

"How old was he? Aubrey's boyfriend?"

North said grimly, "Not legal, I can tell you that much."

"Someone should have called social services," Margot said.

"Nah. He was a hustler. A teenaged hustler. He'd have just run away again. And maybe he was running from something a lot worse than Aubrey."

"Do you remember his name?" Jason asked. It was a long shot at best. There was a good chance that kid hadn't even made it to adulthood, let alone managed to preserve the print of an obscure movie he'd have had to have a 35mm film projector to watch on.

"No," North said. "Micky? Mikey?"

"Did he have a last name?"

"I'm sure he did, but I'm not even sure of his first name. I might be getting him confused with someone else."

"What about a photo of him? Any chance of that?"

"No. I moved around a lot back then." North's smile was sardonic. "I tried to be a real tough guy on the screen and off. Thought it was safer. I wasn't much for keepsakes and forget-me-nots."

CHAPTER SIXTEEN

Sam phoned a little after ten on Thursday night.

"Hey. How was your day?" His voice had that smooth two-whiskey-sours timbre.

Jason pressed Send on the final email of the day, and admitted, "More busy than productive. How was yours? Are you still in Wyoming?"

He'd had not-quite twenty-four hours to sort through his feelings after that strange phone conversation with Sam Wednesday night, and he had come to terms with the reality that, despite their relationship, he was no more privy to the inner workings of Sam's mind than anyone else.

It was a little jarring to face that fact, but Jason had gone into their relationship with his eyes open. Sam was who he was. Jason was who he was. Compromise was the name of the game.

"As a matter of fact, I'm on my way to LA."

"*LA?*" Jason couldn't hide his surprise. But then he remembered. "Right. The task-force-cum-symposium." It made sense. The LA Field Office had headed the original Ripper investigation.

"Do you have plans for dinner tomorrow night? I think we should be able to wrap things up in time for us to grab a meal together."

Now there was a concession. That was the first time Jason could remember Sam hoping to wrap work up early so he could dine with Jason.

Jason's happiness faded. "Hell. I do have plans."

"Of course you do," the whiskey sour said. "Something you can cancel?"

"Unfortunately, no. It's work."

"Well, damn." There was a little bit of that Wyoming cowboy in Sam's voice, though Sam had never been a cowboy. "Any chance of an after-dinner drink?"

As if there was a question that Jason wanted to get together?

"We could meet back at my place? I should be home not much after midnight."

"Late hours for a work meeting," Sam commented.

Jason didn't laugh, but that was kind of funny. Sam knew full-time agents worked fifty-hour workweeks and were on-call 24/7, including weekends and holidays. Safe to say, more than a few evenings were spent away from home and the fam. Hell, Sam's workweek was more like seventy hours.

Sam was not insecure, but every so often he showed an unexpected flicker of jealousy, so it was better to get everything out on the table.

Jason explained about the invitation from Alex to attend the cinephile club as his plus-one, and why he felt this social gathering could be important to his case, especially following Alex's comment about something being awry with the club even before Georgie had made her allegations against Eli Humphrey. The ringing silence on Sam's end of the conversation was a little unnerving, but he managed—barely—to stop himself babbling about the vital work film preservationists did or admitting he'd much rather have dinner with Sam. The more he talked, the more he sounded like he was feeling guilty about something, which he was not.

Or at least, *should* not.

"That's quite the coincidence," Sam drawled at last, and Jason was in no doubt as to which coincidence Sam was referring to.

"I guess it is." He added honestly, "It's a lucky coincidence for me."

"I see that."

"So? Tomorrow night at my place?" There was no reason to be nervous, but Jason had the sudden uneasy suspicion that Sam was going to change his mind about hooking up.

Which made no sense. They were not teenagers struggling through their first crushes. And yet, he braced for bad news.

"Tomorrow night," Sam said. "I'm looking forward to it."

The relief was surely as silly as the nervousness had been, but real all the same.

"Are you spending the weekend?"

"The symposium runs through Saturday." Sam hesitated. "I might be able to wrangle Saturday night. I can't promise."

"Even getting Friday night is…so great. I was thinking it was going to be weeks before I saw you again."

For some reason, the sincerity of that seemed to catch Sam off-guard. "Yeah. I miss you," he said gruffly.

When they'd first settled into the rhythm of nightly phone calls, Jason had tried to push for FaceTiming, but Sam had resisted, saying he preferred to close his eyes and listen to Jason's voice. That it felt closer somehow. It wasn't possible to argue with that, but this was one of those phone calls where he'd have liked to be able to see Sam's face. To see the expression in his eyes.

"I'll see you tomorrow night," Jason said. "I love you."

Sam said so quietly, so seriously, Jason's throat tightened, "I love you, West."

The dial tone that followed was the loneliest sound in the world.

It wasn't until later, as Jason was on the verge of sliding into sleep, that he remembered Sam hadn't said a word about why he'd decided to go hiking at Vedauwoo.

In the end, Jason didn't have to chase Professor Bardolf down.

When he walked out of the ARCS elevators Friday morning, he found Bardolf pacing up and down outside his office.

Spotting Jason, Bardolf put away his pocket watch and called, "Hey, I want to talk to you."

Jason, who'd been on the phone with Charlotte, warning her to make sure Horace made himself scarce that evening, dropped his phone in his pocket. "Good. I want to talk to you too."

"Pop says you're a cop."

"Pop?" Jason swore inwardly. Right. Pop MacIntyre. The geriatric security-guard-slash-maintenance-man-slash-resident-busybody. Jason's suspicion had been right: Pop had eavesdropped on at least part of Jason and Bern's conversation.

"Pop heard Bern promise complete cooperation in your investigation. What *exactly* do you think you're investigating?"

God. Damn. It. Bardolf was making zero effort to keep this conversation confidential. They could probably hear him upstairs in Powell Library.

"Why don't you step inside my office and we'll talk about it?"

"You're damned right I will!"

Fortunately, it was still early, and no other employees had arrived yet. Even Pop was conspicuous by his absence.

All the same, whatever was left of Jason's cover was now officially blown.

He unlocked his office door, and Bardolf charged past him, snarling, "The fact that Bern would agree to work with the cops against his own colleagues!"

Jason flicked on the light. "Have a seat, Professor Bardolf."

"This isn't a social call."

Today Bardolf wore a leather vest, tall, fringed moccasin boots, and a wide brimmed hat with a braided band. All that was missing was his rootin'-tootin' six gun.

"Suit yourself." Jason set down his case, took the chair behind the desk, and leaned back. He studied Bardolf quizzically. "Do you have some reason to be afraid of the police?"

Bardolf mimicked Jason's polite tone. "No, I don't have *some reason to be afraid of the police.* I want to know what the administration is up to, planting a cop on the faculty. This is a blatant violation of Academic Freedom."

"I'm not a cop."

"You're sure as hell not an academic."

Jason's lip curled. "And I don't give a flying fuck about what you say inside or out of the classroom. I'm not here for you. Unless you had something to do with Georgie Ono's death."

"*Georgie?* What are you talking about? What the hell does this have to do with Georgie?" Maybe it occurred to him what it had to do with Georgie because, though it was hard to tell in the unflattering fluorescent light, Bardolf seemed to turn gray. "But the case is closed..." Whatever he read in Jason's expression caused him to fold onto the chair next to the desk.

Jason said, "Professor Ono's family's having trouble reconciling the circumstances of her death."

"What circumstances? It was an accident. What else would it be?"

"Suicide?"

"No way," Bardolf said with absolute certainty. "Never."

"Murder?" Jason suggested.

"*Murder?*" Bardolf gaped. "Who would— That's *ridiculous.*"

"When was the last time you saw Professor Ono?"

"How the hell many times do I have to go through this? I would *never* have harmed her. What would my motive be?"

"If you could just answer the question, sir?"

"Like you don't already know what my answer is? This is bullshit harassment."

Jason opened his mouth, and Bardolf said, "Fine! For the millionth time! I had dinner with her Thursday night. She left my place Friday morning. My neighbors saw her drive away."

"And you went out of town when?"

"I left Friday evening. I returned Tuesday. I didn't see her again after she left my house."

Bardolf had never varied from his account. He did not vary now.

"The neighbors heard you arguing Thursday evening."

"And they also heard us fucking afterward, which is what we always did. We fought and we fucked. We had a passionate relationship."

Jason said, "Was that night a reconciliation? You two had broken up, correct?"

"Broken up?" Bardolf looked taken aback. "We weren't a couple. We weren't *romantic*. We were friends with benefits, and I assure you, the benefits were terrific. I've never had a more satisfying sexual partner." He said with what seemed to be genuine regret, "I can't imagine I ever will again."

Okaay, then. Bardolf's version of their relationship matched no one else's. And yet, while Jason didn't much like the guy, his words had the ring of truth.

Obnoxious truth, but truth all the same.

"You're saying Professor Ono wasn't in love with you?"

"In-in-in love with *me*? Georgie?" Bardolf practically sputtered at the idea. "Georgie was not in love with *anyone*, least of all me. Her *love* was reserved for silver halide crystal ghosts moving across a thirty-foot movie screen in a dark theater."

Alex had said Bardolf knew Ono better than anyone else. Maybe he was right.

"You knew Professor Ono for a long time."

"Is that a question? Yes. I knew Georgie for nearly a decade. We were friends for nearly a decade."

"I see. Well, speaking of movie screens, did Professor Ono ever mention a film called *Snowball in Hell*?"

Bardolf looked surprised. "Where did you hear about that?"

"Georgie told her grandfather she believed she'd discovered a lost noir masterpiece."

"*She* didn't discover it. She was attempting to buy it from the person who discovered it. But the deal fell through. The seller got cold feet."

"Do you know who the seller was?"

Bardolf moved his head in negation. "No. I tried to get the name, but Georgie didn't trust me not to cut her out of the deal." He smiled a foxy kind of smile. "I can't say she was wrong. That film belongs in the archive. Anyway, I think it might have been someone she met on the internet. She was very active in chat rooms and forums."

"Calida Lois believes the person was someone here on campus."

Bardolf shook his head. "She doesn't know what she's talking about. Someone on campus would have come to *me*. I'm the expert. I'm the one with the connections."

Jason gave that viewpoint some consideration. He thought an argument could be made either way. "Is it possible the film didn't really exist? That it was a scam and Georgie was targeted because she had made her interest in that particular film well known?"

"No. The film was real all right. Anyway, Georgie's obsession with *Snowball* began *after* she was approached by the seller. The more she learned about the production, the more determined she was to get her hands on that print."

"Even so—"

"She showed me a film strip: six frames, exposed onto safety stock, from the original film. I've seen what's available on YouTube and in the archive, and these frames were unique."

"What happened to the film strip? It's not in her effects."

"The seller demanded it back after they changed their mind about parting with the film." Bardolf glared at Jason. "You said you're not a cop. Then what are you?"

Jason drew his ID out and offered it—with what Sam would have considered *theatrical flare*. Bardolf, predictably, turned red with anger. "A fed! That's ten times worse! This is all about Eli, isn't it?"

That surprised Jason. "No. It really isn't."

"The hell. Eli didn't try to sell Georgie an illegal copy of *Snowball in Hell*."

"I didn't think he did."

"I don't know what got into Georgie. I don't know why she turned on Eli. But she burned *a lot* of bridges when she went to the cops. I *told* her there was nothing illegal going on. It's a cinephile club, for chrissake. Like she didn't *know* provenance was going to be an issue with films that old and that rare?"

"From what I gather, Professor Ono was very concerned with copyright infringement."

"We're *all* concerned. Of course. That she would take it upon herself—"

"I can see how her decision to go to the authorities might upset a lot of the members."

"We don't have *a lot* of members. We're a select group of friends privately sharing films from our collections."

Jason refrained from comment.

"Georgie was invited in because *I* vouched for her. *I* could have been banned too. She didn't even consider that. A lot of those films will come to the archive one day. It's vital that I remain on good terms with these people. I tried to tell her, but once she got a bug in her bonnet, there was no getting it out. And then, after they kicked her out, she was *wounded*. I asked her, *What the hell did you* think *would happen?* Then she started making threats!"

"Who did she threaten? You?"

"Me? No! Just…everyone. In general. As if that would help reconcile anyone to anything. As if she hadn't already done her worst."

Had she done her worst, though? According to Hick, Georgie's original complaint had started out vague and quickly became downright murky. She had backpedaled. Yes. She had burned bridges, but she hadn't taken down the entire edifice.

Someone surely knew that.

Jason said thoughtfully, "Would you say Professor Ono was a good judge of character?"

Bardolf actually laughed. "She was a *terrible* judge of character. She had no grasp of human nature. She didn't understand how people work, which is why she thought she could turn someone in to the police and still be welcome at his home." Bardolf shook his head. "The truth is, Georgie didn't like people all that much. She preferred the characters in her life to be fictional."

CHAPTER SEVENTEEN

Friday evening, J.J. finally phoned as Jason was dressing for dinner at Eli Humphrey's.

"Guess who's coming to dinner?"

Jason pulled on a black silk T-shirt and tucked it into his black jeans. He studied his reflection in the guest-room mirror. The result was stylish if a little sinister. He answered briskly. "Sam. He phoned last night."

"Oh, right. Well, he's taking the whole team out to dinner." By *team*, J.J. presumably meant the members of the Roadside Ripper symposium.

"Nothing like serial killers to give everyone an appetite."

Jason, already running late, began the inevitable search for his missing boot. How was it possible in a room this size to lose a fu— *Ah*. There it was. In the closet.

"Yeah." J.J. cleared his throat. "So, anyway, the reason I couldn't get back to you earlier was that George Potts had me sit in on the—" He stopped. Tried again. "Do you want the good news or the bad news?"

Jason zipped his boot, straightened, and sighed. "The good news." He was pretty sure what the "good" news *and* the "bad" news were.

Very rarely did J.J. worry about other people's bad news, but he gave another of those uncomfortable throat scratches. "Unfortunately, my good news is more bad news for you."

"Russell, will you spit it out?"

J.J. blurted, "Guess what? I'm back on the Ripper taskforce!"

Jason absorbed that for a moment before offering a doubtful, "Congratulations?"

"Hell yeah, it's congratulations. Being selected for this taskforce is a *major* career coup."

Funny, it hadn't been a coup when J.J. had been partnered with Adam Darling. But Jason held his tongue. He got it. Adam and J.J. had basically been stuck on morgue patrol. Being handpicked by Sam Kennedy to represent the LA Field Office on the new and improved Ripper taskforce was a very different thing.

"Better you than me, buddy."

"You?" Russell laughed at the very idea, which was a little annoying, but not unfair given that Jason had zero desire to be anywhere near a serial killer taskforce/symposium/circle-jerk.

Okay, not fair. It's not like Sam was putting together this symposium of the stars for fun.

"Which means, unfortunately, I'll be taking part in the symposium all weekend." Russell actually sounded apologetic. "So…"

"I'm on my own," Jason finished. "It's okay. I knew this was coming. George hinted this morning he was going to have to reassign you."

"It's not really a reassignment. The symposium will be over on Monday. We can pick up from there. The taskforce isn't going to take all my time. Even if it does, Kennedy's dead set on closing this case *now*. Once and for all."

"Right." Jason appreciated J.J.'s unexpected show of loyalty, but from here on out, he was not going to have a spare minute.

"And now that we know Berkle had an accomplice, it's just a matter of time before we nail him."

"Is that for sure? Berkle had an accomplice?"

"Maybe *accomplice* isn't the right word. Colleague? Collaborator? They shared kill logs."

Jason opened his mouth, then closed it. Russell shouldn't have shared that intel. Likely, the only reason he had was Sam and Jason's relationship.

Into his silence, J.J. said with rare diffidence, "I was pretty sure Kennedy detests me. In fact, I didn't think there was a chance in hell he'd have me on the taskforce again. Did you say something to him?"

Jason smiled sourly at his reflection. "He wouldn't care what I had to say. You're on the taskforce because you were on the original taskforce with Adam Darling and because George has confidence in you. You earned your place on the team, Russell."

"Right?" J.J.'s normal cockiness reasserted itself. "But listen, I do have news on our case. I got the forensic review of Ono's autopsy, and according to the pathologist, the bruising Ono sustained was far more likely to have occurred during that previous altercation than it was during sex play."

"Which is what we thought."

"Yes. But there are marks on Ono's throat not inconsistent with fingernails clawing at the cord around her throat."

"Not   inconsistent?   Meaning   consistent?   Not inconclusive?"

"It's conclusive enough that the ME is changing cause of death from Accidental to Undetermined."

"Yes?"

"Yes. So that's basically it. Right? That's what the senator wanted."

"It's a start, yes."

"It's enough to get LAPD to take another look at the case. Between the two of us, we've come up with more than enough to warrant some follow-up."

It wasn't that simple, of course. Kapszukiewicz would make the call on whether to take this new information to the state attorney.

Jason said slowly, "True."

"It seems to me like our work is done. It's not our job to solve her damn murder."

Again, J.J. was correct. They were not in the business of solving whodunits. The scope of their case was narrow: review LAPD's investigation and advise as to whether there had been missteps or shortcuts or oversights.

That sensation of the rug being pulled out from under him? That was the rug being pulled out from under him. Or at least his investigation.

"Maybe I'm missing something," J.J. said. "But is there anything really left to do but write the report and hand it off to Kapszukiewicz?"

No. Not really.

"There are a couple of loose ends I want to follow up on first," Jason said.

"Uh, the last time there were a couple of loose ends you wanted to follow up on, you wound up being used for target practice in a basement. Remember that?"

It was uncharacteristically tactful of J.J. not to mention what else had happened when Jason had decided to ignore the parameters of his investigation. Jason had not forgotten, and he was not about to risk getting called back on the carpet.

Jason sighed. "You're right. I'll do this dinner tonight and wrap things up at the college tomorrow."

"Jesus, take the win, West."

"Yep. Thanks." He added, "Enjoy your dinner."

"I plan on it." J.J.'s voice faded out, then came back. "Oh. By the way."

"Hm?"

"You're wrong about Kennedy not caring what you have to say. It's in his eyes when you walk into a room. For one split second, he *almost* stops wishing everyone on the planet was dead."

J.J. was laughing as he disconnected.

* * * * *

"You owe me one," Alex informed him when Jason climbed into Alex's Nissan Leaf at a quarter after seven.

"I'm not arguing that which *you*." Jason fastened his seat belt.

Alex threw him a quick, reluctant smile. "Nice. *Joe Versus the Volcano.* You *do* occasionally take time off for a movie. It's not *which*, though. Mr. Waturi says *with*. Repeatedly."

G-Force held Jason silent as Alex shifted into hyperdrive and they shot out of the UCLA faculty parking lot onto Wyton Drive.

"Anyway," Alex continued as they turned right on Woodruff, "BB phoned this afternoon to warn me you were FBI."

Jason threw him a quick look. "Why would he want to warn you in particular?"

"Oh, he wanted to warn everyone. He started with me because Pop told him that you and I were cozy."

"Hell." Pop was a one-man Emergency Communication System.

"This is where you owe me. I talked BB into holding off telling anyone else. I convinced him that your only concern is whether someone murdered Georgie—which should be all of our concern. I swore to him that you were not after anyone's film collection. That you were not concerned with piracy or copyright violation. That you would not jeopardize his position at the archive. I gave him my word, so if you're lying to me—"

"I give *you* my word that I'm not lying to you. I'm not after anyone's film collection. I'm not concerned with piracy or copyright violation." He added, "I can't say that would always be the case, but my investigation is strictly focused on what happened to Georgie Ono."

Alex nodded, his attention on the road ahead. "I also per-suaded BB not to come tonight." He spared a look for Jason. "When he drinks, he talks. And he's still angry. So it's better for both of us if he doesn't show up."

"Thanks. I mean it. I appreciate it."

Alex nodded grimly.

The drive to Eli Humphrey's Beverly Hills mansion took slightly less than ten minutes. The sunlight was just starting to fade as the house came into view.

Humphrey lived in a French-style château surrounded by velvety lawns and manicured shrubs. Jason was familiar with the neighborhood. In fact, it was less than a mile away from Stately West Manor, where he'd lived his entire life until heading off to college—literally less than three miles from home.

That move, though initially viewed by his overinvolved family as surely only symbolic, had been the real deal. He had never again lived under his parents' roof. Not because he didn't love them (he dearly loved them), but because he was determined to forge his own path in the world.

Which he'd done—taking into account all the advantages that naturally came with being born into the wealth and privilege of a political dynasty. None of that interested him, but he didn't pretend it hadn't made a difference.

"Nice house," he commented as Alex zipped up the curving driveway and skillfully maneuvered his electric compact between a Miata and a Mercedes.

"Meh. It's okay," Alex said. "If you don't mind travertine floors, hand-painted frescos, and a small home theater."

Jason sighed sadly. "Sometimes you just have to make do."

Alex grinned, then said, "I'll introduce you, but anything beyond that is above my pay grade."

"Don't worry. I'm not expecting to have to shoot our way out of here tonight. I just want to meet the infamous Mr. Humphrey for myself."

Alex rolled his eyes. "You really are barking up the wrong tree there. Eli is the quintessential fusty old collector."

That could be true. But once upon a time Eli Humphrey had also been an indie film distributor, which meant he had connections and resources highly useful to someone in the business of pirating films.

"We've all got our little secrets."

"You sure do."

"Is there a Mrs. Humphrey?"

"No. But I don't think Eli is gay." A moment later, he said, "He's got a room devoted to his collection of vintage Schaubach Kunst Porcelain. Not my thing, but those figurines go for a pretty penny."

Jason arched his brows. "And you don't think he's gay?"

Alex made a face but declined to answer.

Jason said thoughtfully, "I'm no expert on porcelain, but that Wallendorf Schaubach Kunst stuff rings a bell. Naked kids frolicking with baby goats. Is that right?"

"Those would be cherubs, and they're not what interests Eli, if that's what you're implying. He's strictly into scantily clad blonde ladies. Scantily clad *grown-up* blonde ladies."

Jason smiled. "Point taken."

"I hope so." Alex opened his door, and they got out.

The balmy summer evening smelled of smog and citrus and, very distantly, the wild fires up north. Yellow roses and small coral myrtle flowers were in bloom as they walked past the stone urns topped with greenery and into a small portico. A maid answered the door and led them across yards of pecan hardwood floors and travertine tile through French doors back outside to a wide courtyard covered in rustic brown and yellow pavers and surrounded by bronze wrought-iron railings. Weathered bronze standing lanterns threw aureoles of golden light across the bricks. In the background, a tall waterfall splashed soothingly into a saltwater swimming pool as another uniformed maid circulated a tray of drinks among the four or five men chatting with each other.

Right off the bat, Jason recognized Steve Dugan. Dugan was Peter West's financial advisor and regular tennis partner. Seeing him here was an unpleasant surprise, but given Dugan had to be reintroduced to Jason every year at the Wests' annual Christmas party, Jason was reasonably confident this old family friend wouldn't recognize him out of context.

The maid paused before them with the cocktail tray. Every cocktail was of a different color and in a different type of glass.

Jason glanced at Alex, who said, "You pick what looks good. You'll probably never get the same drink twice."

That was different, but kind of fun. Jason picked a rocks glass filled with pale gold fizziness and a slice of lime. He took a sip of what turned out to be lime, ginger beer, and rum. A Dark and Stormy. Kind of apropos?

Alex selected something tall and blue. "Let me in introduce you to everyone." He nodded in the direction of a reedy, kindly-looking man with thinning white hair and wire-rimmed spectacles. "That's Eli."

As though feeling their gaze, Eli Humphrey turned their way. His vague features rearranged themselves into beaming welcome. "Alex! You made it."

As Alex and Jason walked over to say hello, Humphrey made some aside to the man with him, and the man laughed and nodded.

There was something vaguely familiar about Humphrey's companion. He was medium height, stocky, deeply tanned, and had close-cropped platinum hair. Jason couldn't quite place him. Maybe it was the dark sunglasses. Or was his hair different?

"I wouldn't miss it." Alex smiled at the man with Humphrey. "Hello again."

"And who might you be?" Humphrey turned his mild blue gaze on Jason.

Humphrey's companion was sizing Jason up with a faint, knowing smile.

Jason smiled back. He knew that smile. He knew this guy. But who the hell was he?

Alex was saying, "Eli, this is my friend Ja—"

"Jack," Jason cut in firmly, offering his hand to Humphrey. "Jack Danto." He twinkled at Alex, who looked a little confused but thankfully didn't say a word. "What a *lovely* home you have, Mr. Humphrey!" He giggled inanely.

"It's so nice of you to join us tonight, Jack," Humphrey said. "Alex, you remember Shep? Jack, this is my good friend, Shep."

"Delighted to meet you, Jack," Shepherd Durrand said.

CHAPTER EIGHTEEN

Jason had only met Shepherd Durrand once.

The meeting had taken place back in February at the Fletcher-Durrand gallery, and had only lasted about ten minutes. Given that Jason had looked quite different—well, hell, they had *both* looked quite different—he was pretty sure Durrand didn't recognize him.

Pretty sure, but not certain, and for a few seconds, his heart pounded as he calculated what, if discovered, his move should be.

Hell, if *not* discovered, what should his next move be?

Durrand was wanted for questioning in New York, but no warrant had been issued. Partly, that had to do with the wealth and influence of the Durrand family. Partly, it had to do with the fact that criminal charges had yet to be filed. The evidence against Durrand was largely circumstantial, barring the accusations of a confessed murderer looking to cut a deal. Cape Vincent Police had declined to file charges until they could question Durrand. Durrand had managed to avoid questioning, ostensibly on advice of his legal counsel, then later because he'd left the country.

Now he was back. The platinum dye job and Hail Caesar haircut pointed to Durrand's concern a warrant might be issued once law enforcement realized he had returned to base, but Jason's case had fallen apart and Durrand's most serious crimes had occurred in New York.

Jason smiled, shook hands, and following the old adage that the best defense was a good offense, cocked his head and asked, "Have we met?"

Durrand hesitated, admitted, "You do look rather familiar."

Jason preened. "I do a lot of modeling."

"I believe that!" Durrand responded with automatic gallantry.

Humphrey watched their exchange with a tolerant smile, but Jason couldn't help thinking that despite the Uncle Wiggily overtone, there was something hard in his eyes. Granted, after the experience with Georgette Ono, he was probably wary of guests of guests.

The four of them chatted pointlessly for another minute, and then Alex said, "Come meet the others before dinner." He drew Jason away. "What's going on?" he asked under his breath as soon as they were out of earshot.

"Shepherd Durrand. How well do you know him?"

"Not well. I know *of* him. He doesn't come that often."

"He's wanted for questioning in connection with several murders."

Alex stopped walking. "*Shep?*"

Jason warned, "Don't turn around."

"That can't be right. Shepherd Durrand? Of Fletcher-Durrand?"

"Crazy, I know. He's a complete psychopath. Don't ever let him get you alone. I'm serious. Now, forget about that for a—"

"*Forget* that? You're kidding."

"No. I'm not. I don't want to spook him. Introduce me to the rest of the gang. When I can, I'm going to slip away to make some phone calls."

Alex shook his head in disbelief. "Also, you should have warned me ahead of time you planned on using a stage name."

"I didn't plan on it." Jason grinned widely at a short, stolid-looking man in his thirties who seemed to be glaring at them. "Jack Danto, how're you doing?"

"Kurt Forbes." Kurt shook hands briefly. He scowled at Alex. "I see how it is."

Alex's, "*Kurt,*" sounded pained.

"Actually, we're just good friends," Jason said.

Kurt turned his back on them.

"Oops," Jack Danto said. Jason grimaced in apology. Alex shook his head.

"What's the story with Kurt?" Jason asked as they moved away. "Should I ask?"

"We went out a couple of times. End of story. For me. For Kurt, it was the start of something big."

Jason nodded absently. He felt a little sorry for Kurt. There was nothing more painful than not having your feelings returned. Then he remembered that Sam was actually in Los Angeles, having dinner with his taskforce at this very minute, and that in a few hours they'd be together again.

Aside from the misstep with Kurt, the rest of the cinephile supper club members were perfectly friendly and welcoming. Jason chatted with Steve Dugan about tennis, talked baseball and Shohei Ohtani with an elderly ex-cop named Riley Linnetz, and regretted Bardolf's absence with acting coach Oliver Salah. He listened to all of them talk movies. New movies. Old movies. Bad movies. Good movies. People talking during movies. Especially people talking on their phones during movies.

He remembered what Alex had said about "something being off," but as far as he could tell, there was nothing remotely sinister about any of these guys. Not including Durrand and Humphrey.

In fairness, there was nothing overtly sinister about Durrand and Humphrey either. Yes, Durrand was a psychopath, but he didn't *read* psychopath. He read charming, wealthy ne'er-do-well. And sure, Durrand and Humphrey kept mostly to themselves, and there seemed to be a lot of whispering going on, but that could just be two old friends who hadn't seen each other in a while. There wasn't anything Jason could really put his finger on. He was going by instinct.

Instinct told him, yes, something was up with those two. Maybe it had to do with him. Maybe Durrand had recognized him? Maybe Humphrey had heard something through the grapevine? Maybe Alex hadn't been able to cut Bardolf off in time?

Or maybe they too had good instincts.

When Jason could finally slip away, he headed straight for the lavishly appointed guest bathroom on the first floor. He flipped on the sink taps, phoned Hick's work number—and got his answering machine.

Seven fifty-five on a Friday evening. Even someone as dedicated as Hickok had to give up and go home sometimes.

Jason scrolled through his contacts. He thought he had Hick's home phone somewhere, but it didn't seem to be in his cell phone's address book. He felt for his wallet and realized, to his irritation, that he'd left it locked in the desk drawer at his office. He tried Hick's work number again, and this time left a message.

"It's 7:57 on Friday. On the off-chance you get this, Shepherd Durrand is back in town. He's currently at Eli Humphrey's. I'm going to try to contact Cape Vincent PD, but no way are they ready to rumble. The strongest evidence against Durrand is the Kerk homicide. I don't know if the DA is still hesitant to file charges, but Durrand has changed his appearance, so *he* thinks charges are pending."

Maybe, hopefully, Hick would remotely check his messages one last time that evening, but would he be persuaded to act? That was the question.

Jason turned off the water and returned to the patio.

Alex gave him a look of inquiry. Jason shrugged.

After the drinks tray made a second round, the party moved to a vine-covered pavilion on the far side of the pool. Dinner was served on a long rustic table illuminated by bronze lanterns. The meal, which was very good, consisted of spicy corn carbonara paired with zucchini ricotta galette, roasted artichoke salad, and *a lot* of wine.

The conversation returned to films, and Jason listened absently. Now and then he could feel Durrand looking his way, but he was careful not to return Durrand's attention. Durrand didn't seem nervous or uneasy. He seemed to be enjoying every minute of his evening.

After dessert—a decadent concoction of lavender ice cream, palm seeds, sweetened red beans, shaved ice, fresh strawberries, and toasted coconut flakes in a tall glass—they moved as a group to Humphrey's home theater to watch the 1932 Sherlock Holmes film *The Missing Rembrandt*.

The film was not quite ninety minutes long and was the second in the Holmes series starring Arthur Wontner as the sleuth of Baker Street. The plot revolved around the theft of a Rembrandt painting by a drug-addict artist, and it was pretty convoluted. Sadly, from Jason's perspective, it had a lot more to do with blackmail and lost love letters than the recovery of a lost Rembrandt.

About ten minutes into the film, Humphrey and Durrand silently left the theater.

Jason weighed whether to follow. His desire to know what they were up to warred with his fear of alerting Durrand to the fact that law enforcement had noted his return.

After all, there was no reason to suppose Humphrey and Durrand were "up to" anything besides needing a break from dialog like:

"You would not call me a marrying man, Watson?"

"No, indeed!"

"You'll be interested to hear that I'm engaged."

"My dear fellow! I congrat—"

"To Milverton's housemaid."

"Good Heavens, Holmes!"

"I wanted information, Watson."

"Surely you have gone too far?"

Just because Humphrey was a friend of Durrand's didn't automatically make him a confederate.

Still.

After about five minutes of debating with himself, Jason pretended his cell phone was vibrating, apologized to Alex, and ducked down so as not to block the screen on his way out of the room.

As the door of the home theater closed behind him, he spotted Humphrey striding down the hall toward him. He was alone.

Jason smiled vaguely, scrolling through his messages. "It's like they always know the worst time to call," he said to Humphrey.

Humphrey smiled politely. Behind the round spectacles, his milky eyes were cold. "I'm terrible with names. Who did you say you were again?"

Jason stopped scrolling and dropped his phone in his pocket. "Jack Danto."

"And you're a friend of Alex's?"

"We haven't known each other long. I'm teaching film studies at UCLA."

"I see." Humphrey nodded at some private thought.

"Did Shep leave before the end of the movie?" Jason asked innocently.

Humphrey pursed his lips. "I think he'd guessed the ending."

"That's a shame. Sherlock Holmes is always full of surprises."

"Only if you're very new to the oeuvre." Humphrey offered another chilly smile and went into the theater. He let the door swing shut behind.

"*Oeuvre*," Jason murmured. "Damn." He gave it a minute and slipped back inside.

"**Y**ou can see why BB is a little defensive," Alex said on the quick drive back to UCLA.

Jason had offered to drive. Despite the quantity and quality of wine, he'd had very little to drink. But Alex, possibly out of unease at what Jason might do, had also restricted his alcoholic intake, and declined.

"Why?" All day long Jason had managed to keep his attention where it needed to be: On The Job. But in a short while he'd be seeing Sam, and despite the frustrations of the evening, he couldn't contain that rising swell of happiness. He just wanted to grab his car and get home as soon as humanly possible.

"Eventually, that film's coming to the archive. Unless something gets in the way."

"That film was terrible," Jason commented.

Alex threw him a quick look of disbelief. "I thought your gig was art preservation. Conservation theory needs to *embrace* transience."

"No question." But in the very act of choosing what to preserve and when, there was inevitably curation. And curation, like critique, was subjective.

There was a short silence.

"Theoretically, *The Missing Rembrandt* is a lost film," Alex said. "I don't know where or how Humphrey got a copy, and I don't think the print we saw was complete, but getting that film safely into the archive will be a coup for BB."

"I imagine so." Jason asked curiously, "How did you get to be part of this film clique?"

"BB and I go way back. I started out as a film studies major."

"What happened?"

Alex smiled faintly. "There's a lot of variety and possibility in a BFA. I'm a movie geek. I didn't necessarily want to make my own movies, and I sure as hell didn't want to have to try to compete in the cutthroat environment of the film industry. I just wanted to do art for a living, which I feel like I do."

"Did you ever hear of a film called *Snowball in Hell*?"

"No." Alex glanced his way. "Why?"

"Professor Ono didn't discuss her attempts to acquire the film with the rest of the club?"

"If she did, it wasn't when I was around. I've never heard of it."

"It was gay noir flick from the 1950s."

Alex was shaking his head. "No such film ever existed. No way. *Victim* didn't come along until 1961. The Brits were way ahead of us there."

"No, it really was made. I've seen snippets of it on YouTube. It's officially listed as a lost film."

"And *Georgie* found it?"

"Sort of. Maybe. An anonymous seller approached her with what seemed to be frames from the original film. She showed the film strip to Bardolf, and he thought they were genuine."

"He never mentioned it."

"He was hoping to cut her out and obtain the film for the archive."

"That sounds like BB. What happened with the film?"

"The seller changed their mind."

Alex was silent for a moment, then said, "Do you think Durrand recognized you?"

"I don't know if he recognized me, but he knew something was up." Jason smothered a sigh. It had been a long day and a long evening. "I guess you don't survive decades as a psychopath without developing a keen sense of danger."

"That's...yeah. I mean there were rumors of legal problems at the gallery, but I never dreamed the Durrands were the subject of an FBI investigation. And Shep. I mean, yes, there's always been something sort of...slithery about that smile of his. He shakes hands too long. But..."

Jason said, "The people who were there tonight. Aside from Bardolf, is that pretty much everyone?"

Alex made an unamused sound. "It's funny you should mention that. Yes and no. BB would usually be there. Some of the more elderly members..."

"Ran out of daylight?"

"How noir of you. But yes. And we do have people show up and then fade out. Or at least, I used to think they dropped out, but now and again, I get the feeling there's another...membership tier."

Jason studied Alex's profile. "That's very interesting."

"Another thing I've been thinking lately is that it's kind of odd Georgie was our only female member. Ever. There are no women in that club."

"I noticed that," Jason said.

"**W**ell, it's been real and it's been fun," Alex said as Jason got out of the Nissan.

Jason's moonlit rental was the only other vehicle in the faculty parking area.

Jason leaned down, grinning. "But it hasn't been real fun?"

"Actually, it was pretty fun. You're…quite the catalyst."

"I've been called worse."

"And probably were, after we left." Alex's smile was rueful. "I'll see you Monday, I guess?"

Jason hesitated. "I probably won't be here on Monday. I think my investigation has pretty much run its course."

"Oh." Alex's smile faded. "That's—well, I guess good news, really. Depending on what happens next. I've enjoyed—it was nice seeing you again."

"Thank you so much for your help, Alex." Jason offered his hand. "I mean that. I know you had mixed feelings about… things. And one thing that won't happen next is my breaking my word to you."

They shook hands.

Alex said, "Thanks. I appreciate that."

"Take care." Jason closed the car door and tapped the roof in goodbye.

The Nissan Leaf glided slowly, silently away.

CHAPTER NINETEEN

Jason considered leaving his wallet until the following day when he'd be tidying up the final odds and ends of his investigation at the college, but no. It wasn't only his credit cards. His credentials case was in there.

He was a little curious about something else as well.

Most nights there was plenty happening on the UCLA campus: movie screenings, concerts, plays, lectures, sports, of course, and kids just generally fooling around. But on Fridays the research and study center closed at five and the library at six, so at this hour the grounds near Powell were quiet and museum-like as Jason used his access card to enter through the security door.

He was quick and quiet, moving through the shadows of the columns on the reading-room floor. All empty buildings were a little eerie at night, especially a building the size of a small castle. The uncertain light flickered across the suspended ceiling with its mystical stars and ceiling beams. The scent of books, old and new, perfumed the air with dry notes of wood and leather and dusty vanilla. Weird that even after-hours, you could almost hear whispers and the *flip* of pages.

He reached the elevators and punched the button for the basement. He stepped inside. The doors closed. He glanced at his watch.

Sam would be at the bungalow, and Jason was eager to get home. The phone was better than nothing, but he was longing to look into Sam's eyes. To touch Sam. To have Sam touch him.

The elevator doors opened on disconcerting darkness.

Not total darkness. But tomblike enough to be momentarily disorienting. The only illumination came from the overhead emergency lights, and that faint green glow added to the general horror-movie atmosphere.

Jason moved soundlessly down the narrow corridor, past the row of locked doors. Despite the shortage of space on campus, most of these closet-sized offices remained unoccupied. For one thing, despite its proximity to Powell Library, this was pretty much off the beaten path. For another, it had all the comforts of an underground bunker.

His nostrils twitched at the smell of cleaning supplies and that odd acidic odor that seemed to permeate the walls. That was vinegar syndrome, the chemical reaction resulting from the deterioration of cellulose acetate. Or, in layman's terms, it was the scent of old movies dying.

He glanced over his shoulder. He didn't hear anything and certainly didn't see anything to make him think he was not alone, and yet…the feeling that he was not alone persisted.

"Hello?"

Silence.

"Pop?"

Silence.

Jason reached his office, let himself inside. His skin prickled with unease. He unlocked the desk drawer, grabbed his wallet and credentials, and stepped back into the narrow hallway. Out of the corner of his eye, he caught movement and ducked just in time as something whistled through the air, barely missing him as he jumped sideways and drew his weapon.

He found himself facing… Pop.

Pop, glasses glinting blindly, hair on end, holding a broomstick like a weapon—or the proverbial ten-foot pole.

"What the hell?" Jason exclaimed.

"What are you doing here this time of night?" Pop sounded both outraged and frightened.

"I left my wallet."

Pop's face scrunched into an expression of disbelief.

Jason held his weapon on Pop for another moment, then shouldered it. He wasn't entirely surprised. In fact, he'd kind of suspected Pop might be sleeping sometimes in one of the unused offices.

Pop was protesting, "Then you should have left it for tomorrow. You have no business down here after hours."

"Do you?"

"Do I what?"

"Have business down here at eleven thirty at night."

"I don't report to you," Pop said scornfully. "It's none of your business when I choose to come to work, mister."

Jason considered the broom still positioned to hold him at bay. He considered Pop's rumpled uniform and ruffled hair. He considered Pop's genuine fear and anger.

He tried to make his body language less threating, put his hands out, palms up. "Look, Pop, I think you and I got off on the wrong foot."

Pop took a wary step back. "You think so, do you? Maybe that's because I know a ringer when I see one."

"A ringer?" Jason smiled. "What do you think I'm a ringer for?"

"Don't give me that. You're a cop. I can smell a cop from a mile away."

"I guess I need a better brand of soap," Jason said, "because I'm not a cop."

"That's how a cop argues. What you're really saying is, you're a *fed*. I hate feds worse than I hate cops!"

"Why?" Jason was genuinely curious. If Pop was employed by the university, he couldn't have much of a criminal record. Granted, not everyone who detested law enforcement had a criminal record. Disconcerting though it was, some perfectly law-abiding citizens bore contempt for the agencies intended to protect and support them.

"You ever hear of Evan Foreman?"

Jason hesitated. The name was vaguely familiar. He couldn't quite place it.

Pop continued to give him that glittery glare. "I guess you're too young to remember the film raids of 1974 and 1975 when the FBI, the DOJ, and the MPAA tried to wipe out all the indie film dealers and film collectors."

"What the hell's the MPAA?"

Pop threw him a look of disbelief. "You ever hear of the Motion Picture Association of America, dumbass?"

Ouch. Okay, fair enough. Jason had been thinking an obscure division of—well, it didn't matter.

"And you pretend to be a film studies professor!"

"*American International Pictures, Inc. v. Foreman,*" Jason said. "Got it." Not the Bureau's finest moment for sure, being used as a tool for the studios in their shameless battle to extend and reextend copyrights on films that long ago should have slipped into public domain.

"That's right," Pop said. "Copyright was intended to be a protection for artists for *a limited time.* It wasn't supposed to be used by greedy corporations to gouge generation after generation of moviegoers long after the film makers are dead and gone."

Pop clearly had powerful feelings on this subject. Maybe that came from listening to archivists for decades? Maybe it was something else? Just because someone had strong opinions about copyright duration didn't automatically make them a pirate. Plenty of people in no danger of being put to death had strong feelings on the death penalty.

"I agree with you," Jason said. "What's happening now with copyright was never the original intent of the law. It doesn't benefit the original artist or the public."

Pop stopped ranting and scowled at Jason. "We wouldn't even *have* some of these films in this archive if it wasn't for collectors."

"I know. I don't disagree."

The truth was, about a third of 35mm movie prints still in existence owed that existence to the film collectors and dealers labeled "pirates" by the very studios that had shown no interest in preserving the same films.

"And I find that very suspicious!"

Jason hung on to his patience. "I can see the difference between pirating copies of the latest *Harry Potter* and showing a bootleg print of *The Gold Bug* filmed in 1910."

"Sure you can. You just want to have a nice friendly chat about borrowing a copy of your favorite movie, and then BLAMMO!"

Jason winced at that shouted *Blammo.* "Sorry? Blammo meaning…what?"

"You slap the bracelets on." Pop held up his wiry wrists as though showing off his new set of handcuffs.

Jason knew better than to laugh. "That would be entrapment. Pop, how long have you been working here?"

"Longer than you've been on this planet, mister."

"I'm older than I look."

"You look like you're thirty-four."

"You've been working in the archive for thirty-four years?"

"I've been the night watchman here since 1976."

"Since the early days. But you're here most days as well. What exactly do you do?"

Pop said aggressively, "Whatever needs doing."

"Okay, sure. What do you like best about your job?"

Pop glared, folding his arms like a genie about to take back all Jason's wishes. "I don't have to talk to you. I know my rights."

Jason sighed. He just wanted to go home and see Sam. Was that too much to ask?

"You're right. You don't have to talk to me. It's okay if you don't trust me. But I'm not here to investigate film piracy or copyright violation."

In fact, were that the purpose of his investigation, the UCLA film archive would be the last place he'd look.

"Then why *are* you here?"

Did it matter now?

Jason said, "Honestly? Professor Ono's family felt the investigation into her death was rushed. I was asked to take a look. That's all."

Pop was silent. The thick spectacles masked his features in a Kafkaesque blankness.

"Did you know Professor Ono? I understand her office was down here."

Jason still wasn't sure if that had been Ono's choice or Bern's attempt to keep her from riling her colleagues. The more he came to know about Ono, the more he suspected it had been her choice.

Pop jeered, "Did I *know* her? You mean, did we socialize? A professor and a security guard? No."

"But you must have occasionally spoken to her. *Good morning. Good night. Nice weather we're having.* What did you think of her?"

"I thought she was a professor and I was a security guard."

Jason studied Pop. Pop stared back defiantly. There were several questions Jason would have liked to ask, but it was clear that Pop was not going to answer. Not here and not now.

Maybe later? Maybe after he'd had some time to think? Maybe after they'd both had some sleep?

"Well, thanks for your time. Sorry for disturbing you."

Pop lowered his broom. He still seemed guarded, but also a little surprised.

Not relieved. Surprised.

What had Pop expected to happen?

Jason thought about that in the elevator on his way up to the library.

Yeah, it wasn't his imagination. Something about Pop just didn't feel right.

Maybe Pop had legitimate reason for being afraid of law enforcement. Maybe Pop really did have something to hide.

* * * * *

Charlotte must have managed to get hold of Horace because there was no sign of the security guard when Jason parked beside Sam's rental car in the narrow drive behind the bungalow on Carroll Canal.

He got out, and the summer night smelled of bougainvillea, warm cement, and the dank, dark scents of the canal. Telephone poles buzzed overhead, and one of the alley lights flickered on and off.

Jason unlatched the wooden gate at the side of the house and went through.

The side door porch light shone in welcome, casting a warm glow over the brick patio. Through the kitchen windows, Jason could see Sam standing at the sink, sipping a drink.

His heart rose, a wave of happiness rolling through him like high tide on a spring morning.

Sam left the window, and the kitchen door opened as Jason reached it. He stepped inside, Sam's arms folded around him, and for a long minute they just held each other, not saying anything.

It was the best feeling in the world to have Sam's arms around him again. To feel Sam's heart beating against his own. To hold Sam tight. He never wanted to let go.

But of course he had to let go. He had to say something. He muttered, "It feels like forever."

"It does." Sam's voice was quiet.

"How the hell are we going to do this? Go *weeks* without seeing each other?" He hadn't meant to launch into it, hadn't meant to say it at all. He had agreed to these terms, gone into this with his eyes open. He hadn't realized how hard it was going to be.

Sam shook his head, didn't answer.

Because what was there to say? There was no solution to this. Or at least, not a solution either of them could contemplate.

Jason expelled a long, only slightly shaky breath, drew back, and smiled. "Wow, it's nice coming home to you." He tried—hoped—he sounded cheerful.

Sam raised his hands to Jason's face, studying him.

Sam's expression was so grave, so intent, Jason's smile grew uncertain. He was expecting, waiting for Sam's kiss, for that hunger and heat to claim him, but instead Sam continued to cup his face.

"Your hair," he said softly.

"Camouflage."

Sam breathed a half laugh, murmured, "You can't hide from me, West," before leaning in to touch Jason's mouth with the gentlest of nuzzles.

Jason's breath hitched, his heart thumped loudly in his ears as Sam's tongue slid across his lower lip, moist, tantalizing, unexpectedly soft.

Arousal washed through Jason, swept him along, drowning all thought, drowning everything but longing for Sam's mouth, Sam's body, *Sam*.

He locked his hands behind Sam's head, feeling the soft crispness of his hair, the hard outline of skull, the tension of muscles in his neck and shoulders, and drew Sam's head down.

He whispered, "I don't know if I ever told you this, but I really, *really* love you."

"Yeah?" Sam whispered back.

Jason nodded.

Their mouths touched again, delicately, lightly, then fiercely, Jason's eyelids quivering beneath that delicious assault of lips and tongue. His bones seemed to dissolve, and he clutched Sam's shoulders, feeling the shudder that rippled through him, absorbing that little earthquake into himself.

"Christ." Sam groaned. His hands ran caressingly down Jason's back, clenched his buttocks, hiking him up.

Jason moaned in response, wrapping his legs around Sam, lost in the dark, moist sweetness of Sam's mouth. He was absently aware they were maneuvering past the dining alcove with its pale-blue sideboard and padded benches, shuffling across toward the white settee in the living room, vaguely conscious when hardwood gave way to terracotta tile.

They tumbled onto the settee, Jason fumbling for the fastening of Sam's jeans, Sam groping for Jason's waistband. There seemed to be a forest of hands and dicks to work through before Jason finally, with a gasp of relief, was free of the constraint of clothes. Sam pushed Jason's hands aside, yanked his own jeans and briefs down, and his cock sprang free.

Sam's erection was huge, notable for size and color and weight, the scent of mown grass—that would be the Escentric Molecules Molecule 03—and imminent sex. His hands clamped on Jason's buttocks, and he began to thrust against him.

It was hot and rough and Jason was already cresting—even the dampening recollection that Horace might be wandering somewhere outside couldn't stem the tide.

He threw his head back, crying, "Oh fuck, fuck, Sam. Oh, oh, oh…*yeah, baby*!"

A funny laugh tore out of Sam, but he didn't break rhythm, didn't lose the plot, muttering, "Slow down, West. Christ…"

It's not a race. Jason had heard that before.

Maybe it always *felt* like a race because they had so little time together. One of them always having to grab the phone, catch a plane, catch a bad guy.

Sam changed his grip, grew caressing, cherishing, stroking Jason's chest, sternum, belly, smiling grimly at Jason's little gasps and gulps.

He said quite seriously, "You're my favorite thing in the world, West."

Jason laughed, but honest to God. He didn't seem to need more than this: Sam saying something funny and the hot, swollen press of genitals. He didn't seem to need much more than Sam.

Sam reached between their bodies, gently cupping Jason's balls, as though relearning them. Jason opened his mouth to Sam's tongue as Sam began to thrust against him, harder, faster. Jason arched up, and holy moly, that was an awkward angle…

It happened without further preliminaries, the orgasm simply bubbling up and spilling over, that uncorked *welcome home, welcome back, welcome to anything I have*, leaving them both gulping for air, spent and shaking and soaked right there on the too-small settee.

For long, shuddering moments, Jason lay slumped against Sam, listening to the quick *thump* of Sam's heart, the *splash* and *swash* of people on the canal—even at midnight—a car rolling down the alley behind the house, tires grinding gravel, the drapes sighing against the open window.

Sam's arms were warm and supportive. Jason tipped his face up, and Sam was smiling faintly, eyes closed.

"Thank God for Scotchgard," Jason said, and Sam opened his eyes.

They both started laughing.

CHAPTER TWENTY

"Did you ever think of teaching?" Jason asked.

It was later, technically Saturday. They had moved to the bedroom, to the comforts of mellow lamplight and a welcoming mattress, and were drinking *Anijsmelk*, hot milk flavored with aniseed and sweetened with honey. Anna, de Haan's girlfriend, had sent Jason a couple of packets of *anijsblokjes* as a thank-you gift, and it seemed like the perfect nightcap since both he and Sam were working the following day.

Sam said, "Teaching? No. I don't have the patience to teach."

"I don't think I do either. I thought I did. I always thought teaching would be something I could fall back on, if I had to." Jason smiled. "Like Indiana Jones. His day job was professor of archaeology."

"His day job was being Indiana Jones. Teaching archaeology was his cover. Anyway, you're substitute teaching. It's not the same as it would be teaching subjects you know and love."

Jason acknowledged that with a little grimace. He set his empty mug on the nightstand, folded his arms comfortably behind his head. "What do you think you'd be doing if you hadn't gone into the FBI?"

This was potentially sensitive territory. Sam had gone into the FBI after Ethan had been murdered. He had been a man on a mission.

Sam sipped his drink, seeming to think it over.

"Rich rancher?" Jason suggested.

"Rancher?" Sam looked taken aback. "Me?"

It looked like maybe Ruby had gotten that one wrong. Or, more likely, Sam had changed a lot from that tow-headed second grader hoping to even the score.

"Fireman? Astronaut?"

"I was going to be a criminal psychologist." Sam took a mouthful of spicy milk, considered, swallowed. "Now I think I'll just marry money." He winked at Jason. He was not a winker.

"Be careful," Jason warned. "I might take you up on that."

"You can take me up on that." Sam's gaze held his. "I assume you will eventually."

"Sure. How's that going to work with each of us on opposite sides of the country?"

"One of us would have to compromise."

And when you say one of us...

"Isn't that what we're already doing?"

And when I say we...

Sam said, "It's not possible for me to do my job across country."

"I know."

"There isn't an ACT in the country that wouldn't jump at having you onboard."

"That's not true. For one thing, there aren't ACT openings anywhere right now. Even if there were…"

"You wouldn't want to leave LA." It wasn't a question. Sam's voice had a note of finality.

Jason did not want to leave LA. That was true. But the reasons he didn't want to leave wouldn't mean much to Sam. Sam had no problem living eighteen hundred miles from his mother. In fairness, Sam's mother was a lot younger than Jason's parents. Jason had been a surprise baby, arriving after his sisters had reached adulthood. His parents were healthy but elderly.

Jason loved his little house by the canal. Sam was as equally at ease living out of a hotel room as at his Stafford, Virginia apartment.

Jason liked and valued his LA team members—well, the point was, Jason didn't want to move. It was to his advantage professionally and personally to stay right where he was. But the long stretches of separation were killing him.

Even Sam seemed less than content.

"You know," Jason said, "last time we talked about this—in this very bed—you told me you weren't sure moving in together was a good idea."

"I'm not sure it's a good idea," Sam said. "I'm just sure *not* moving in together is a fucking terrible idea."

That was the most vehement Sam had been, and it was a balm on Jason's sore heart. He moved into Sam's arms again, and Sam lifted his mug to avoid baptizing Jason in Anijsmelk.

Jason listened to the strong, steady *thump* of Sam's heart. It was nice like this. Pleasant. He was relaxed and happy. He didn't want to do anything to break the mood, but he had to know.

"You never told me why you went hiking at Vedauwoo."

Sam grunted. His version of *ugh.* "It's not a bedtime story."

Jason raised his head to study the hard lines in Sam's face. "I still need to know."

Sam studied him without expression.

Finally, he said, "It looks like Berkle and our unsub met three times over the course of their...careers. On those occasions, they exchanged notebooks. Kill logs. The last batch of those was still in Berkle's possession when he died."

"So all the victims were attributed to Berkle?"

Sam moved his head in assent.

"Were they working together?"

"No. It doesn't appear so. We're not sure how they connected, but they seemed to have been in contact for a very long period. They compared notes, learned from each other, which is why so many of their kills seemed to share a signature. There's a lot more that we don't know than what we do know. What we do know..."

Was terrifying.

Sam didn't say that, of course. The monsters didn't terrify Sam, though maybe they should have.

Jason said slowly, "You no longer think Ethan was murdered by the Roadside Ripper."

"We have—had—two Roadside Rippers."

"You don't think Berkle killed Ethan."

Sam said flatly, "I think Ethan was killed by someone living in Wyoming."

Jason sat up. "You think Bone Road *lives* in Wyoming?"

"Yes. There are drawings, sketches in Bone Road's note-book that indicate to me he wasn't just passing through."

"Sketches of Vedauwoo? In connection with Ethan's murder?"

"It's the way it looked to me."

Jason stared at Sam's impassive features. "Did you find what you were looking for?" His mouth felt dry. "Ethan's grave?"

No. That didn't make sense. Ethan's body had been found.

Or had it?

Sam shook his head. "No." He added, "I'm not sure that's what I was looking for. We don't have a roadmap with names and dates. We're trying to piece together the visual clues of one offender showing off for another offender. Some of the original notes and drawings were altered, embellished later on."

Jason thought that over. "What if Ethan is still alive?"

Sam's expression grew bleak. "Ethan's not alive."

"Are you one hundred percent sure the body you identi-fied as Ethan *was* Ethan?"

"As sure as I could be, given the state of the remains."

"For the sake of argument, what if he was alive?"

Sam shook his head.

Which was not the most reassuring response. Did that mean *so what*? Or *you're out of your tiny mind*? Jason was silent, watching Sam work through it.

Sam said suddenly, as if it had only occurred to him, "Are you— Do you think Ethan turning up alive would have any-thing to do with you and me?"

"How could it not?"

Sam's expression was so… In fact, Jason couldn't make sense of that expression.

Sam said crisply, "First of all, if Ethan was alive and let me go on thinking he was dead all these years, let his father think he was dead all these years, he was never the person I thought he was. Secondly, Ethan and I were… I don't know we'd still be together. That was decades ago. We were practically kids. We didn't have a hell of a lot in common then. What would we have in common now? We'd be strangers."

"It doesn't mean you wouldn't—"

Sam cut right through that. "Thirdly, I loved Ethan. Yes. But what I felt for Ethan was—it isn't comparable to what I feel for you. Do you still not understand that?"

The answer was right there in Sam's eyes, and so was Sam's exasperation. The funny thing was, the more reassuring emotion was the exasperation.

"Yes. I do. But you can't deny there would be, I don't know, unfinished business?"

"Some business finishes by default whether through time or circumstance. In this case, we have both time and the circumstance of *you*."

"I appreciate that, and I'm not pushing for—I'm not even sure what I'm trying to say. It's just that this is the guy whose death changed the direction of your life. Obviously, you have to have some feeling about—"

Sam said wearily, "And you're the guy whose life is changing the direction of my life." He put his mostly untouched milky drink on the nightstand. "We should sleep. Tomorrow's going to be another busy day." He pulled the chain on the blue-green Tiffany lamp by the bed, plunging the room into hazy moonlit gloom.

Sam hiked his shoulders more comfortably against the pillows and sighed.

That weight-of-the-world sigh got to Jason. He shifted, put a protective arm around Sam. Sam responded, wrapping his arm around Jason. They settled against each other and made peace with small, soft kisses.

"No. Not child pornography." Sam was definite.

Jason argued, "How can you be so sure?"

They were on their way out the door early Saturday morning, laptop cases slung over their shoulders, travel coffee cups in one hand, car keys in the other.

Sam gave him a look of disbelief. "This is what I do, remember?"

"Right, but—"

"I'm drawing conclusions based on what you've told me. The personalities you've described. The scenario you've detailed. You're not dealing with pedophiles. This is not a child pornography ring."

Jason locked the side door to the bungalow and joined Sam on the brick walkway. "But films are part of it. Watching films for sure. Probably distribution."

"Snuff," Sam said succinctly.

Jason stared.

Sam was bleak and brisk as a December churchyard. "Given what we already know of Shepherd Durrand? I don't think there's any question. You're dealing with snuff films. A snuff film ring. Something small and exclusive. Not another Wonderland Club. The victims will not be children. And this is not happening over the internet. This will occur in real time, up close and personal. These are people with a lot to lose. They will be very cautious in who they permit into their inner circle. They will lawyer up immediately."

As rare as snuff "art" films were, snuff film distribution rings were even rarer—though there had been a couple of highly publicized international busts in 1998 and 2000. However, as Sam pointed out, given what they knew about Shepherd Durrand and his extracurricular activities, masterminding a snuff film ring was easily within his wheelhouse. In fact, it was the most likely explanation for Ono's ever-changing charges against Eli Humphrey with LAPD, as well as Alex's suspicion that there was another tier of membership at the cinephile club.

It also confirmed Jason's instinctive unease on meeting Eli Humphrey. Nice to know his creepy factor receptors were in working order.

Sam interrupted Jason's thoughts. "Phone Jonnie and bring her up to speed on Durrand. This is one of the missing pieces in our case."

"Will do." He was more amused than offended at Sam throwing orders at him like he was his PA. He got it. This was a big development in the BAU's investigation into Shepherd Durrand. It was possibly a major break in Jason's investigation as well. If Ono had somehow discovered this particular interest of Humphrey's—and Humphrey knew it—it gave him a strong motive for wanting her out of the way.

Granted, nothing much seemed to have come from Ono's concerns, partly because she'd backtracked after approaching the police. Per Hick, she'd started out with a complaint regarding unspecified illegal materials, which eventually turned into pirating copyrighted materials.

In fact, Jason needed to talk to Hick as well as Jonnie. But busting a snuff film ring was not going to fall to the FBI's Art Crime Team *or* LAPD's Art Theft Detail. This one belonged to Violent Crimes. Jason and Hick would play their roles, but they would not be the ones slapping on the bracelets.

That was acceptable to Jason. So long as someone managed to bring down Durrand, he could live with it. He'd sure as hell like to be there, though.

Sam, having delivered his pronouncement, was already on his phone and headed for the wooden side gate. Jason opened his mouth to ask if Sam knew yet whether he was staying over in California, then shut it. Clearly, he was dismissed.

His smile was derisive and aimed at himself. A tiger couldn't change its stripes, but you had to give it credit for trying. He glanced up at the wall of bamboo and tropical banana palms. The banana trees were in bloom, and their sweet, fruity fragrance filled the morning air. He realized this was the first time he and Sam had been together that he hadn't grilled Sam about Jeremy Kyser.

The truth was, you could get used to anything, if you tried.

Speak of the devil, Hick phoned Jason's cell as Jason started down Carroll Canal. Sam's G-ride loan was a yard or two ahead, Sam still on his phone, addressing the troops. Jason noticed the two-story contemporary on his left was once again officially up for rent. Which could be good or bad news. The last tenants had owned a cockatiel that kept escaping into Jason's backyard. He'd had to "rescue" the damned bird twice, and both times it had tried to bite him. But that could still be preferable to someone who played lousy guitar all night.

"GOA," Hick said bitterly. "Gone On Arrival. We're still trying to get the warrant. He didn't go back to his place last night, and he's not at the gallery. As far as anyone can tell, he's in the wind."

Jason swore. "Could he be headed back to New York?"

"I don't think so. Maybe? There was a falling out between him and big brother Barnaby after everything that went down on the island. Plus, Cape Vincent PD have more on him. Not that they want to use any of it."

Jason brought Hickok up to date on recent events, including Sam's theory that Durrand had probably partnered up with Humphrey in a snuff film ring.

"Jesus Christ. Is he going for Gotham City Villain of the Year?"

Jason watched Sam's vehicle turn and disappear around the corner. "I mean, this is a weirdo who used his art gallery as a torture chamber, so I don't think we should be surprised."

"Okay, well, this changes everything," Hickok said grimly. "I've got to kick this upstairs ASAP."

"I figured."

"You've got a knack for walking into the lion's den, West."

"Fools rush in," Jason said.

"Does this mean you're pulling up stakes at the college?"

"Yes. Even before Durrand entered the game, I thought another look into Ono's death was probably warranted. That's what my report will say."

"I've got to admit, I feel bad about writing the lady off as a crank. I wish she'd just come out and told us what she thought was going on."

"If she didn't have proof, and she probably didn't, she'd have been afraid of being laughed out of your office. I mean, if Shepherd Durrand wasn't a player in all this, *I'd* have trouble buying it. For years I thought snuff films were strictly urban legend."

Hickok said, "Ono didn't seem like someone to back down in a fight, but if she went up against Durrand, she'd never know what hit her."

"I agree," Jason said. "The MO is pure Durrand. The way her death was staged? It's got his fingerprints all over it."

"Too bad not literally," Hickok said.

"It'll different now that you guys know what you're looking for. Someone will talk."

"Someone always does," Hick agreed.

CHAPTER TWENTY-ONE

Hugo Quintana was waiting when Jason arrived in the Touchstone lobby to collect his belongings from Professor Ono's apartment.

"You didn't fool me. I knew you were a cop the whole time," Quintana informed him, following Jason into the elevator. "I could smell it on you."

"I'm starting to get a complex," Jason remarked. "If you knew I was law enforcement, why have you been such an ass? I'm just doing my job. Same as you."

Quintana puffed up like an angry rooster. "Same as me, right!" His laugh was harsh. "Don't bother with the fraternal order bullshit now. If you wanted cooperation, you shoulda been upfront about why you were here. Your pal with the Bob's Big Boy do was replaying LAPD's greatest hits."

"Meaning?"

"They wanted to blame it all on us. They hinted we were harassing her and ignoring break-ins. Or *we* were the ones trying to break in. We were negligent, or we were criminal. Take your pick. Their minds were all made up. I know how cops think, how they look at security personnel: rent-a-cops, toy cops, plastic badges, wannabe cops. I've heard it all. From cops! Anybody gets hurt, it *must* have been our fault. We weren't doing our jobs."

Jason got it. Security guards, prison guards, they *didn't* get a lot of respect. That didn't mean they didn't have a tough job or weren't doing it to the best of their ability.

"You have to admit there were some gaps in protocol," Jason said. "Erasing the security camera film every forty-eight hours, for one. Allowing unmonitored access into the building after ten o'clock at night. Those were procedures that needed to be corrected. But if it makes you feel better, there was nothing in the police reports to indicate suspicion fell on any member of Touchstone's security team."

"No, just the team as a whole!"

Jason inwardly sighed. He was wasting his breath. Quintana had a chip on his shoulder the size of a prison ball. In his defense, he'd been the target of Ono's accusations, so maybe that touchiness was understandable.

They reached Ono's apartment. Quintana insisted on waiting in the hall as Jason went inside and gathered up his files and belongings. It didn't take long. He had a final look around. Even after a week of sifting through the circumstances of Georgette Ono's life—and death—he had no strong sense of who she was or what she had wanted.

When I went to the film and saw all the black-and-white feelings that nobody felt...

But maybe the idea that anyone ever really knew anyone else was a comfortable illusion. Certainly, a career in law enforcement would lead you to that conclusion. Trust in another person was both calculated risk and leap of faith—even for the Sam Kennedys of the world.

He stepped into the hall, let the apartment door close behind him. Quintana stuck his hand out, and Jason handed over the keycard.

"It's all yours."

But in the elevator on the way down, Quintana's curiosity got the better of him.

"*Was* she murdered?"

Jason shrugged. "It looks like it."

"Do you know who did it?"

"I think so. Proving it will be up to someone else."

Quintana folded his arms as though this kind of half-assed answer was exactly what he expected.

Jason was nearing the UCLA campus when he noticed a battered gold Chevy Impala in his rearview.

The Impala was a couple of lengths back, and he was unsure when he'd picked it up—or *if* he'd picked it up. There was more than one vintage gold beater tooling around the mean streets of LA. Maybe this was the same car that had nearly run him down in Touchstone's front driveway. More likely not.

Still.

As he neared the entrance to faculty parking, Jason began to plan out where he would position his vehicle, his communications to UCLA's security personnel and campus police, the condition of his carry—he had managed to stop compulsively checking his weapon every time there was a chance he'd have to fire it (a tic he had picked up after his shooting in Florida), but he always felt a flash of anxiety that he was unprepared for the worst.

He was not unprepared. He was trained, and he was ready.

All unnecessary because as he turned off, the Impala continued down the street, flashing past the gates too fast for Jason to get more than a glimpse of the driver: pulled-down felt hat, hunched shoulders…

The car did not have a license plate.

In the cold light of day—well, the cold light of day did not reach down to the subterranean chambers of the Archive Research and Study Center—but on Saturday morning, with office doors open and slightly hungover employees wandering zombie-like through the narrow corridors, Jason's midnight encounter with Pop felt like just another weird dream.

He let himself into his shoebox of an office, pulled out his computer, turned on Harry Styles, and settled down to work. He was hoping to finish his report and be out of there by lunch.

He was reviewing the crime-scene video of Ono's apartment one final time—the fact that she'd been found hanging in the closet should have been everyone's first clue something was amiss (her family had drawn the obvious conclusion when they'd gotten rid of her mattress)—when Sam phoned.

"Hi!" This was definitely a surprise. By Jason's estimation, Sam should be up to his elbows in grisly forensics and disturbing psych evaluations by now. He lowered the volume on "Late Night Talking."

"Hey."

"How's it going?"

Sam said curtly, "I just wanted to let you know I'll be staying through Sunday. I'll fly out Monday a.m."

"You're kidding."

The silence on the other end of the line was absolute and utter.

"That's *great*," Jason said quickly. "I didn't think— This is *great*."

Sam said, "I get the feeling you believe you're the one making all the compromises."

Jason said carefully, "I think I'm in a position to make more compromises."

"That's correct. But."

"But?"

"We'll talk it over this weekend."

What the hell did that mean? Was this good news or bad news?

"All right. I'm not complaining. You know that, right?"

"I know that. See you tonight. Probably around nine."

"See you tonight. I l—"

"Love you," Sam concluded briskly, and hung up.

Okay, then.

Jason returned to studying the crime-scene vid. Part of why everyone (himself included) had overlooked the unlikelihood of Ono pleasuring herself to death in a closet probably had to do with discomfort over Ono's sexual proclivities as well as the distraction of the pornographic articles strewn around her feet. Had he shown Sam this video, Sam would probably have instantly noticed all the silly inconsistencies—

His email dinged.

Joe North's roommate Margot had emailed him with an attachment.

Jason opened the email. The message was no more than a note.

Joe found this in a folder with some old contracts. Second from the left is David Aubrey's boyfriend. Marty? Hope this helps.

M.

Heart beating in anticipation, Jason downloaded and clicked on the black-and-white photo. Four men on a film set. He easily identified Aubrey and North; both were in costume. He was pretty sure the man to the right of North was director Henry Walsh. Jason turned his attention to the fourth man. Slim and pretty in a waifish way. Also very young. This would be Marty, the teenaged hustler, and Aubrey's boyfriend. Marty had pale hair, horn-rimmed eyeglasses, and gave the impression of watching Aubrey even when he wasn't looking at him.

Was he familiar? Jason tipped his head from left to right, trying to get a better angle. *Do I know you, Marty?* He zoomed in on the photo, zoomed in on Marty's pouty mouth and big, colorless eyes.

"Gotcha." Jason sat back in triumph. He felt validated but also a little shocked as he gazed at Marty AKA Martin MacIntyre AKA Pop. Former guardian and now the ghost of the archives.

An hour later, Jason was still a little shocked.

According to Campus Human Resources, each department was responsible for the maintenance of personnel records for staff employees in accordance with the provisions set forth in UC-PPSM 80, blah, blah, blah.

According to the Campus Security Authority, Martin MacIntyre had retired in 2015.

2015.

That would have been around the time the archives had been moved to Santa Clarita. Around the same time, Tim Pearce, Chair of the Department of Film, Television, and Digital Media—and Aric Bern's predecessor—had also retired.

Was it that simple? Had Pop continued to come to work for the next seven years and *no one noticed*?

Granted, Pop had an uncanny ability to make himself scarce when he wanted to. Like now, when he was nowhere to be found.

Jason called around until he was able to locate Aric Bern at brunch with friends. Bern freely admitted he had no idea of Pop's work schedule. In fact, he was grateful for Pop's devotion to duty. Bern had figured Pop was close to retirement, but had been hoping he might hang on for another year or two.

"C-c-close to retirement!" Jason spluttered. "The guy's gotta be in his eighties."

"Some people don't age well," Bern retorted.

After that, Jason spent some time trying to track where Pop lived. Assuming it was not in a cleaning closet somewhere on campus.

Campus Security's last known address turned out to be a dud. The apartment complex had been torn down three years prior to make way for a shopping complex. Jason managed to find another address through the Social Security Adminstration. That turned out to be a post-office box at Mail and More in Hollywood.

Progress. Sort of.

From there he turned to the DMV. The DMV had the same address for Martin MacIntyre as the Social Security Administration. Also of interest: they listed MacIntyre as the registered owner of a 1962 gold Chevy Impala. It got better. In 1966, the car's registration had been transferred from a David Aubrey to MacIntyre.

Jason absorbed that information with little surprise. By now, he thought he had a pretty good picture of how Professor Georgette Ono had come to learn about what was perhaps the only existing copy of *Snowball in Hell*—and why that knowledge had proved fatal.

But why the hell would Pop have gone so far as to kill Ono? She couldn't have forced him to give the film to her.

Did Pop understand that?

Ono was not good at taking no for an answer. Had she threatened him?

With what?

Jason sat up straight and stared at the scratched and battered door of his temporary office. Had Ono, naturally suspicious and perhaps looking for leverage, done a little looking into Pop's background? Perhaps his employment record? Had she discovered Pop's secret? Had she threatened him with exposure?

You didn't have to be Sam Kennedy to understand how Pop would react to losing his—imaginary—position at UCLA.

Nor was it hard to believe that one person Ono would open her door to, no matter what the hour, no matter what she was doing, was the person in possession of *Snowball in Hell.*

Nor did Pop need to know anything about Ono's sexual habits in advance. Suppose, after he'd killed her, he walked into her bedroom, and saw what she'd been up to? You wouldn't have to be a master criminal to recognize the advantage of using existing props in order to rearrange the scene to look like suicide.

Case closed?

Well, no, not really. But yes. Kind of.

Since no federal crime had been committed—no piracy, no copyright infringement, no art moved across state lines or sold internationally—no federal statute applied, so Jason would be handing everything he had over to LAPD. Assuming their findings matched his own, it would be up to the local Assistant District Attorney to prosecute.

All that remained was for Jason to finish his report, phone Kapszukiewicz and, with her permission, contact Senator Ono.

By the time Jason left UCLA, it was after five.

The blue sky was fading, and the late-afternoon sun cast a hazy golden sheen over the trees and towers growing small in his rearview mirror. The traffic was light, and he was content.

The call with Kapszukiewicz had gone well. Even better than he'd hoped. He felt…redeemed. More importantly, Kapszukiewicz seemed to believe he was redeemed—or that her faith in him was redeemed. Either way, a weight he had not been aware of fell from his shoulders.

The call with Senator Ono had not gone as well. Or, at least, the old man had cried, and that had been hard to listen to. But Ono had insisted he was glad to know the truth, and Jason believed him. Sometimes the truth was all there was to give.

As he drove, he kept an eye out for the gold Chevy Impala, but there was no sign he was being followed. If Pop had any sense… Well, given the things Pop had done—done and gotten away with—there was no predicting.

And sure enough, when Jason reached Carroll Canal and Court D, he spotted the Impala several houses down, partially concealed behind large green and blue trash barrels.

It seemed he hadn't been the only one spending the day doing research. Although in Pop's case it looked more like reconnaissance. Jason found his phone, dialed 911, provided his badge number, and reported the situation to the Venice Beach substation. He gave the dispatcher a description of the Impala, a description of Pop, and warned that he too would be on scene and armed. Getting shot by local law enforcement would not be much of an improvement over getting shot by Pop.

Not that Pop was necessarily armed. He seemed to favor improvising with whatever was at hand. However, trying to overpower Jason would not be like overpowering a small, unprepared woman. Pop had presumably planned for tackling Jason.

Parking several houses down in the opposite direction from the Impala, Jason got out and jogged back down the secluded alleyway to his bungalow, keeping beneath decks and overhangs, staying in the shadows as much as possible. He was on high alert, his heart pounding, but he kept his weapon low, braced for running into someone walking their dog or carrying the trash out. It was dinnertime, and his neighbors seemed to be busy preparing their meals. He could hear the *clink* of glasses and laughter from porches. Delicious aromas of cooking food mingled with summer flowers and the ripe and dusty scent of the alley. His stomach growled. There hadn't been time for breakfast, and he hadn't stopped for lunch.

Jason reached his side gate. He took a couple of deep, steadying breaths. He did not want to get ambushed.

Was it possible Horace's presence might have scared Pop off?

Or was Horace also wandering around armed and ready to shoot at the *snap* of a twig?

Jason swore softly. His gaze fell on the FOR RENT sign on the house next door.

He crossed the garage beneath the two-story, vaulted the low iron gate, and moved silently—as silently as he could through dead leaves—along the side of the house. He noticed the trash bins against the wooden fence were filled with garbage, which was odd, given the house had been empty for at least a month.

As he moved down the length of the tall wooden fence, he listened closely for sounds of approaching sirens or movement from his own yard. No sirens. He could hear the chimes on the pergola over his walkway, skateboarders on the sidewalk across the canal, a plane droning overhead.

The fence provided more privacy than he'd realized. The best view into his own property would be from the upstairs deck of this house.

Where the hell were the cops?

In fairness, it had probably been no more than four minutes since he'd phoned for assistance. Four excruciatingly long minutes.

There were floor-to-ceiling windows all along the side of the house, but they were fixed picture windows. Jason rounded the corner, followed the hedge-lined walkway to a small wooden deck with a firepit. He crossed the deck, tried the tall glass doors, and was not entirely surprised when they slid soundlessly open.

His heart was hammering against his collarbone as he traveled down the long, unfurnished room. He noted an open-hearth fireplace, built-ins, wooden floors. No sign that anyone had been there in weeks. He ran up the wide, open slat staircase, reached the top level, weapon at ready.

There's no one here. The house is empty.

The house *felt* empty. But the sense of looming menace only grew stronger with each step.

Now Jason could hear the wail of sirens approaching. Far from reassuring, that high howl seemed to spiral with his ever-rising anxiety. He felt like he was moving in slow motion through a nightmare as he crossed the landing into the primary bedroom.

Absently, he was aware of more built-ins, another fireplace, more windows, glass doors leading out onto a balcony.

The scream of sirens echoed off the walls and pavement of the alley behind the house. He registered the *pound* of boots, the *clunk* of body armor, the *crackle* of radios—and the *smash* of his wooden gate going down.

And, more distantly, he heard someone shouting for help.

A thin, hoarse voice crying out from the canal.

"Help! Murder! Help!"

Now what?

Jason pushed out through the glass doors. Something hard and small rolled beneath the sole of his boot. A pebble? He picked it up automatically, strode onto the balcony deck with its picturesque vista of the canal and the expensive homes across the water

He'd been right. The balcony offered a perfect telescopic view into his small, shaded yard. At the end of his yard was a small reedy embankment giving way to the canal. An elderly man was splashing around in the greenish water, shouting.

Pop?

Pop couldn't swim? Or was this a ruse to—

No. In the next instant, Jason realized neither could be the case. The boaters making their way to Pop also began shouting and pointing.

"What the hell..."

Jason leaned over the railing and saw what the commotion was about. The bloated body of a man in a blue security uniform was floating face up in the bloom of yellow algae spreading across the water.

Horace Pratt.

A wave of dizziness swept over Jason. He closed his eyes. The pebble fell from his fingers and bounced on the deck. He gripped the railing hard, drew in long, steadying breaths, got control of himself.

The police had rushed through his yard and were hauling Pop out of the canal. Jason watched as if from a great distance.

Jesus Christ.

He needed to pull himself together, get down there and claim federal jurisdiction for this homicide. No gray area here. Murder in an FBI agent's own backyard? There wasn't a more direct attack on a federal agent than that. The FBI crime-scene investigators would need to process this crime scene. He watched Pop still shouting and pointing. The police were looking around in confusion. Jason whistled sharply. Waved.

As he looked down, something caught his eye. The pebble he'd dropped rested an inch or so from the toe of his boot. He stared, the hair on the back of his neck prickling.

Not a pebble.

A small, round carving.

Netsuke.

A *netsuke* jack-o'-lantern.

ACKNOWLEDGMENTS

Dear Reader-Friends—and especially to all you Bruins out there—this is a work of fiction and NOT a visitor's guide to the UCLA campus. The intent is to entertain, not help you find Melnitz Hall. Many, *many* liberties have been taken with locations, procedures, personnel, you name it, to further the interests of the story.

Note: Most of Jason's Rate My Professor reviews were tweaked from actual Rate My Professor scores.

I want to thank the Academy—oops, wrong. Thank you to the usual suspects: Keren Reed (as ever and always), the SO, my Facebook mods, my Goodreads mods, Emily the Office Elf, my wonderful, supportive Patrons who kept me going during the months I just wasn't able to write.

Thank you in advance to Kale Williams for his narration of the audio edition of this book (because that's how good you are).

Thank you to Johanna Ollila for her so-beautiful, evocative cover art.

Thank you to SamSpayedPI for clarification on the government agency ethical issues and for delivering Jason from a rather sticky situation.

We all love movies. We may not all realize our shared film heritage is in dire straits. Despite the gains of the last few decades, the clock is ticking on many old films and the creative efforts of countless artists and creators. If you'd like to be part of the solution, consider donating to the National Film Preservation Foundation.

Jason West and Sam Kennedy will return.

Keep reading! If you liked
The Movie-Town Murders,
you might like this excerpt from the first book
in the Dangerous Ground series.

DANGEROUS GROUND

Chapter One

The nose of the red and white twin engine Baron 58 was crunched deep into the bottom of the wooded ravine. Mud and debris covered the cockpit windows. One wing had been sheared off when the plane crashed through the surrounding pines, knocking three of them over. The other wing was partially buckled beneath the craft. The tail of the plane had broken off and lay several yards down the ravine.

Taylor mopped his face on the flannel sleeve of his shirt. Ten thousand feet up in the High Sierras, the sun was still plenty warm despite the chill spring air.

Behind him, Will said, "Either the pilot was unfamiliar with the terrain or he didn't have a lot of experience with mountain flying. Out here, avoiding box canyons is one of the first things you learn."

"Take a look at this," Taylor said, and Will made his way to him across the rocky, uneven slope. Taylor pointed to the fuselage. "You see those registration numbers?"

"N81BH." Will's blue eyes met Taylor's. "Now why does that sound so familiar?"

Taylor grinned. "It's the plane used in that Tahoe casino heist last year."

Will whistled, long and low.

"Yeah," agreed Taylor. Just for a moment he let his gaze linger on the other man's lean, square-jawed features. Will's hair, brown and shining in the sun, fell boyishly into his eyes. He hadn't shaved in three days, and the dark stubble gave him a rugged, sexy look—very different from the normal nine to five Will. Not that they exactly worked nine to five at the Bureau of Diplomatic Security.

Will's gaze held his for a moment, and Taylor looked away, focusing on the plane's registration numbers again.

"What'd they get away with again?" Will asked in a making conversation kind of voice. "Something in the neighborhood of 2.3 million, was it?"

"That and murder," Taylor said grimly. "They shot two sheriff's deputies making their getaway." These days he was touchy about law enforcement officers getting gunned down.

"Doesn't look like they got away far." Will moved toward the open door of the plane. He hopped lightly up onto the broken wing, and for a moment Taylor felt a twinge of envy. He was still moving slowly after his own shooting six weeks ago; sometimes he felt like he was never going to get it all back: the strength, the speed—the confidence—he had always taken for granted. He felt old at thirty-one.

He walked toward the broken off tail piece, and Will— only half-joking—called, "Watch out for snakes, MacAllister."

"You had to say that, didn't you, Brandt?" Taylor threw back. He studied the rim of the ravine. It had been winter when three masked men with automatic weapons robbed the Black Wolf Casino on the Nevada border of Lake Tahoe. They had fled to the nearby airport, hijacked a plane, and disappeared into the snowy December night.

Local law enforcement had theorized the Beechcraft Baron crashed in the High Sierras, but the weather and the terrain had inhibited searchers. It was clear to Taylor now that even under the best conditions, it would have been just about impossible to spot the little plane tucked away in the crevice of this mountainside.

He glanced back, but Will had vanished inside the wrecked plane. He could hear the eerie creak and groan of the aircraft as Will moved around inside.

Taylor worked his way around the crash site. Not their area of expertise, of course, but he knew what to look for.

Scattered engine parts and broken glass were strewn everywhere. A couple of seats had been thrown clear and were relatively intact. There was a weathered plank of wood that must have originally been a table or a desk, and some broken light fixtures and vinyl parts of storage bins. The plane could have carried five passengers in addition to the pilot. The casino had been hit by three bandits; the fourth had been driving the getaway car that sped them to Truckee Tahoe Airport. Four people would have inevitably left DNA evidence, but the crash site was four months old and contaminated by the elements and wildlife. He glanced around at the sound of Will's boots on the loose rock.

Will said, "The pilot's inside. No one else."

That was no surprise. The initial investigation had cleared the pilot of involvement in the robbery; if he'd been alive, he would have contacted the authorities. Taylor thought it over. "No sign there were any passengers on board when she went down."

"What about an incriminating black tie?" Will referred to the famous narrow black necktie that legendary hijacker D.B.

Cooper left on the Boeing 727 he jumped out of way back in 1971.

"Not so much as a stray sock."

"Then I guess they weren't doing laundry up there," Will remarked, and Taylor drew a blank.

"You know how one sock always gets lost—forget it." It was a lame joke, but once Taylor would have known instantly what Will meant. Once Taylor would have laughed. "Parachutes?" Will asked.

"No parachutes."

"None?"

"Doesn't look like it," Taylor said.

"Interesting. The pilot's got a bullet through his skull."

"Ah," said Taylor.

"Yep."

Their eyes met.

"Come take a look," Will invited, and Taylor followed him back to the front section of the plane.

Will sprang onto the wing, reaching a hand down for Taylor, and with a grimace, Taylor accepted his help, vaulting up beside him. The wing bobbed beneath their weight, and Will steadied him, hands on Taylor's waist for an instant.

Taylor moved away. Not that he minded Will's hands on him—there was nothing he'd have liked more than Will's hands on him—but this had nothing to do with attraction and everything to do with lack of confidence. A lack of confidence in Taylor being able to look after himself. Not that Will had said so, but it was clear to Taylor—and maybe it was clear to Will too, which might explain what the hell they were doing up in the High Sierras one week before Taylor was officially due to start back at work.

Because if they couldn't figure this out—get past it—they were through as a team. Regardless of the fact that so far no one had admitted there was even a problem.

"After you," Will said, waving him into the gloomy and rotting interior of the plane with exaggerated courtesy. Taylor gave him a wry smile and ducked inside.

"Jesus. Something's made itself right at home in here."

"Yeah. Maybe a marmot. Or a weasel. Something relatively small." Will's breath was warm against the back of Taylor's neck.

"Relatively small is good," Taylor muttered, and Will laughed.

"Unless it's a skunk."

Almost four years they'd been together: partners and friends—good friends—but maybe that was over now. Taylor didn't want to think so, but —

His boot turned on a broken door lever, and Will's hand shot out, steadying him. Taylor pulled away, just managing to control his impatience.

Yeah, that was the problem. Will didn't think Taylor was capable of taking two steps without Will there to keep an eye on him.

And that was guilt. Pure and simple. Not friendship, not one partner watching another partner's back, not even the normal overprotectiveness of one partner for his injured-in-the-line-of-duty opposite number. No, this was guilt because of the way Taylor felt about Will—because Will didn't feel the same. And somehow Will had managed to convince himself that that was part of the reason Taylor had stopped a bullet.

He clambered across the empty copilot's seat and studied the remains of the dead pilot slumped over the instrument dashboard control panel. The pilot's clothes were in rags, deteriorated and torn. Bacteria, insects, and animals had reduced the body to a mostly skeletal state. Not entirely skeletal, unfortunately, but Taylor had seen worse as a special agent posted in Afghanistan. He examined the corpse dispassionately, noting position, even while recognizing that animals had been at it. Some of the smaller bones of the hands and feet were missing.

"One bullet to the back of the head," he said.

"Yep," Will replied. "While the plane was still in flight."

Taylor glanced down at the jammed throttle. "And then the hijackers bailed out," he agreed. This part at least still worked between them. They still could work a crime scene with that single-mindedness that had earned the attention and approval of their superiors.

Not that they investigated many homicides at the Bureau of Diplomatic Security. Mostly they helped in the extradition of fugitives who fled the country, or ran interference for local law enforcement agencies with foreign police departments. But now and then they got to…get their feet wet. Some times were a little wetter than others. Taylor rubbed his chest absently.

"In the middle of the night and in the middle of nowhere," Will said. "Hard to believe all four of them made it out of these mountains safely. FBI and the local law were all over these woods within twenty-four hours."

"Yeah, but it was snowing, remember."

"Those guys are trained."

"They missed the plane."

"The plane wasn't making for the main highway."

"Maybe the bad guys were local," Taylor said. "Maybe they knew the terrain."

"Wasn't the prevailing theory, was it?"

"No." He backed out of the cockpit, and Will did it again—rested his hand on Taylor's back to stabilize him—although Taylor's balance was fine, physically and emotionally.

He gritted his jaw, biting back anything that would widen the rift between them. Will's friendship was better than nothing, right? And there had been a brief and truly hellish period when he thought he'd lost that, so…shut up and be grateful, yeah?

Yeah.

Will jumped down to the ground and reached up a hand. Taylor ignored the hand, and dropped down beside him—which jarred his rib cage and hurt like fuck. He did his best to hide the fact.

"More likely what's left of 'em is scattered through these woods," Will commented, and Taylor grimaced.

"There's a thought."

"Imagine jumping out of a plane into freezing rain and whatever that headwind was? Eighteen knots. Maybe more."

"Maybe someone was waiting for them on the ground."

Will nodded thoughtfully. "Two and an almost-half million divides nicely between five."

Taylor grunted. Didn't it just? Kneeling by his pack, he unzipped it, dug through his clothes and supplies, searching for something on which he could note the crash site coordinates. It was sheer luck they'd stumbled on it this time. He found the small notebook he'd tossed in, fished further and found a pen, pulling the cap off with his teeth. He squinted up at the anvil-shaped cliff to the right of the canyon. The sun was starting to sink in the sky. He rose.

Will moved next to him, looking over his shoulder, and just that much proximity unsettled Taylor. It took effort not to move away, turn his back. Will smelled like sunshine and flannel and his own clean sweat as he brushed against Taylor's arm, frowning down at Taylor's diagram.

"What's that supposed to be? A chafing dish?"

Taylor pointed the pen. "It's that…thing. Dome or whatever you call it."

"If you say so, Picasso." Will unfolded his map. "Let me borrow your pen."

Taylor handed his pen over, and Will circled a spot on the map, before folding it up again, and shoving it in the back pocket of his desert camo pants.

"Well, hell," he said, "I guess we should start back down, notify the authorities we found their missing aircraft."

Will looked at him inquiringly, and Taylor nodded. That was the logical thing to do, after all. But he wasn't happy about it. Three days into their "vacation" they weren't any closer to bridging the distance yawning between them—and it would be a long time before they had this kind of opportunity again. By then it might be too late. Whereas this plane had been sitting here for over four months; would another four days really make a difference?

"Right. We'll rest up tonight and head back tomorrow then," Will added, after a moment.

Taylor directed a narrow look his way, but the truth was he *was* fatigued, and climbing in the dark would have been stupid even if he wasn't. So he nodded again, curtly, and tossed the notebook and diagram back into his pack.

* * * * *

Will was tired. Pleasantly tired. Taylor was exhausted. Not that he'd admit it, but Will could tell by the way he dropped down by the campfire while Will finished pitching their two-man tent.

One eye on Taylor, Will stowed their sleeping bags inside the Eureka Apex XT. He pulled Taylor's Therm-a-Rest sleeping pad out of his own backpack where he'd managed to stash it that morning without Taylor noticing, and spread it out on the floor of the tent. He opened the valve and left the pad inflating while he went to join Taylor at the fire.

"Hungry?"

"Always." Taylor's grin was wry—and so was Will's meeting it. Taylor ate like a horse—even in the hospital—although where he put it was anyone's guess. He was all whippy muscle and fine bones that seemed to be made out of titanium. It was easy to look at him and dismiss him as a threat, but anyone who'd ever tangled with him didn't make that mistake twice.

He was too thin now, though, which was why Will was carrying about three pounds more food in his pack than they probably needed. He watched Taylor feeding wood into the flames. In the firelight his face was all sharps and angles. His eyes looked almost black with fatigue—they weren't black, though, they were a kind of burnished green—an indefinable shade of bronze that reminded Will of old armor. Very striking with his black hair—Will's gaze lingered on Taylor's hair, on that odd single streak of silver since the shooting.

He didn't want to think about the shooting. Didn't want to think about finding Taylor in a dingy storeroom with his shirt and blazer soaked in blood—Taylor struggling for each anguished breath. He still had nightmares about that.

He said, talking himself away from the memory, "Well, monsieur, tonight zee specials are zee beef stroganoff, zee Mexican-style chicken, or zee lasagna with meat sauce."

"What won't they freeze-dry next?" Taylor marveled.

"Nothing. You name it, they'll freeze-dry it. We've got Neapolitan ice cream for dessert."

"You're kidding."

"Just like the astronauts eat."

"We pay astronauts to sit around drinking Tang and eating freeze-dried ice cream?"

"Your tax dollars at work." Will's eyes assessed Taylor. "Here." He shifted, pulled his flask out of his hip pocket, unscrewed the cap, and handed it to Taylor. "Before dinner cocktails."

"Cheers." Taylor took a swig and shuddered.

"Hey," Will protested. "That's Sam Houston bourbon. You know how hard that it is to find?"

"Yeah, I know. I bought you a bottle for Christmas year before last."

"That's right. Then you know just how good this is."

"Not if you don't like it." But Taylor was smiling—which was good to see. Not too many smiles between them since that last night at Will's house. And he wanted to think about that even less than he wanted to think about Taylor getting shot.

"Son, that bourbon will put hair on your chest," he said.

"Yeah, well, unlike you I prefer my bears in the woods."

There was a brief uncomfortable pause while they both remembered a certain naval officer, and then Taylor took another swig and handed the flask back to Will.

"Thanks."

Will grunted acknowledgment.

He thought about telling Taylor he hadn't seen Bradley since that god-awful night, but that was liable to make things worse—it would certainly confuse the issue, because regardless of what Taylor believed, the issue had never been Lieutenant Commander David Bradley.

Taylor put a hand to the small of his back, arching a little, wincing—and Will watched him, chewing the inside of his cheek, thinking it over. It was taking a while to get back into sync, that was all. It was just going to take a little time. Sure, Taylor was moody, a little distant, but he still wasn't 100 percent.

He was getting there, though. Getting there fast—because once Taylor put his mind to a thing, it was as good as done. Usually. When he started back at work he'd be stuck on desk duty for a couple of weeks, maybe even a month or so, but he'd be back in the field before long, and Will was counting the days. He missed Taylor like he'd miss his right arm. Maybe more.

Even now he was afraid—but there was no point thinking like that. They were okay. They just needed time to work through it. And the best way to do that was to leave the past alone.

"Warm enough?" he asked.

Taylor gave him a long, unfriendly look.

"Hey, just asking." Will rose. "I was going to get a sweater out of my bag for myself."

Taylor relaxed. "Yeah. Can you grab my fleece vest?"

Will nodded, and passing Taylor, took a swipe at the back of his head, which Taylor neatly ducked.

* * * * *

They had instant black bean soup and the Mexican-style chicken for dinner, and followed it up with the freeze-dried ice cream and coffee.

"It's not bad," Taylor offered, breaking off a piece of ice cream and popping it into his mouth.

Actually the ice cream wasn't that bad. It crunched when you put it into your mouth, then dissolved immediately, but Will said, "What do you know? You'll eat anything. If I didn't watch out you'd be eating poison mushrooms or poison berries or poison oak."

Taylor grinned. It was true; he was a city boy through and through. Will was the outdoors guy. He was the one who thought a week of camping and hiking was what they needed to get back on track; Taylor was humoring him by coming along on this trip. In fact, Will was still a little surprised Taylor had agreed. Taylor's idea of vacation time well spent was on the water and in the sun: renting a house boat—like they had last summer—or deep sea fishing—which Taylor had done on his own the year before.

"They never did arrest anyone in connection with that heist, did they?" Taylor said thoughtfully, after a few more minutes of companionable chewing.

"What heist?"

Taylor threw him an impatient look. "The robbery at the Black Wolf Casino."

"Oh. Not that I heard. I wasn't really following it." Taylor had a brain like a computer when it came to crimes and unsolved mysteries. When Will wasn't working, which, granted, was rarely, the last thing he wanted to do was think about crooks and crime—especially the ones that had nothing to do with them.

But Taylor was shaking his head like Will was truly a lost cause, so he volunteered, "There was something about the croupier, right? She was questioned a couple of times."

"Yeah. Questioned but never charged." He shivered.

Will frowned. "You all right?"

"*Jesus*, Brandt, will you give it a fucking *rest*!" And just like that, Taylor was unsmiling, stone-faced and hostile.

There was a short, sharp silence. "Christ, you can be an unpleasant bastard," Will said finally, evenly. He threw the last of his foil-wrapped ice cream into the fire, and the flames jumped, sparks shooting up with bits of blackened metal.

Taylor said tersely, "You want a more pleasant bastard for a partner, say the word."

The instant aggression caught Will off guard. Where the hell had it come from? "No, I don't want someone more pleasant," he said. "I don't want a new partner."

Taylor stared at the fire. "Maybe I do," he said quietly.

Will stared at him. He felt like he'd been sucker punched. Dopey and…off-kilter.

"Why'd you say that?" he asked finally into the raw silence between them.

He saw Taylor's throat move, saw him swallowing hard, and he understood that although Taylor had spoken on impulse, he meant it—and that he was absorbing that truth even as Will was.

"We're good together," Will said, not giving Taylor time to answer—afraid that if Taylor put it into words they wouldn't be able to go back from it. "We're…the best. Partners and friends."

He realized he was gripping his coffee cup so hard he was about to snap the plastic handle.

Taylor said, his voice low but steady, "Yeah. We are. But…it might be better for both of us if we were reteamed."

"Better for you, you mean?"

Taylor met his eyes. "Yeah. Better for me."

And now Will was getting angry. It took him a moment to recognize the symptoms because he wasn't a guy who got mad easily or often—and never at Taylor. Exasperated, maybe. Disapproving sometimes, yeah. But angry? Not with Taylor. Not even for getting himself shot like a goddamned wet-behind-the-ears recruit. But that prickling flush beneath his skin, that pounding in his temples, that rush of adrenaline—that was anger. And it was all for Taylor.

Will threw his cup away and stood up—aware that Taylor tensed. Which made him even madder—and Will was plenty mad already. "Oh, I get it," he said. "This is payback. This is you getting your own back—holding the partnership hostage to your hurt ego. This is all because I won't sleep with you, isn't it? That's what it's really about."

And Taylor said in that same infuriatingly even tone, "If that's what you want to think, go ahead."

Right. Taylor—the guy who jumped first and thought second, if at all; who couldn't stop shooting his mouth off if his life depended on it; who thought three months equaled the love of a lifetime—suddenly *he* was Mr. Cool and Reasonable. What a goddamn laugh. Mr. Wounded Dignity sitting there staring at Will with those wide, bleak eyes.

"What am I supposed to think?" Will asked, and it took effort to keep his voice as level as Taylor's. "That you're in love? We both know what this is about, and it ain't love, buddy boy. You just can't handle the fact that anyone could turn you down."

"Fuck you," Taylor said, abandoning the cool and reasonable thing.

"My point exactly," Will shot back. "And you know what? Fine. If that's what I have to do to hold this team together, fine. Let's fuck. Let's get it out of the way once and for all. If that's your price, then okay. I'm more than willing to take one for the team—or am I supposed to do you? Whichever is fine by me because unlike you, MacAllister, I —"

With an inarticulate sound, Taylor launched himself at Will, and Will, unprepared, fell back over the log he'd been sitting on, head ringing from Taylor's fist connecting with his jaw. This was rage, not passion, although for one bewildered instant Will's body processed the feel of Taylor's hard, thin, muscular length landing on top of his own body as a good thing—a very good thing.

This was followed by the very bad thing of Taylor trying to knee him in the guts—which sent a new and clearer message to Will's mind and body.

And there was nothing Will would have loved more than to let go and pulverize Taylor, to take him apart, piece by piece, but he didn't forget for an instant—even if Taylor did—how physically vulnerable Taylor still was; so his efforts went into keeping Taylor from injuring himself—which was not easy to do wriggling and rolling around on the uneven ground. Even at 75 percent, Taylor was a significant threat, and Will took a few hits before he managed to wind his arms around the other man's torso, yanking him into a sitting position facing Will, and immobilizing him in a butterfly lock.

Taylor tried a couple of heaves, but he had tired fast. Will was the better wrestler anyway, being taller, broader, and heavier. Taylor relied on speed and surprise; he went in for all kinds of esoteric martial arts, which was fine unless someone like Will got him on the ground. Taylor was usually too smart to let that happen, which just went to show how furious he was.

Will could feel that fury still shaking Taylor—locked in this ugly parody of a lover's embrace. He shook with exhaustion too, breath shuddering in his lungs as he panted into Will's shoulder. His wind was shit these days, his heart banging frantically against Will's. These marks of physical distress undermined Will's own anger, reminding him how recently he had almost lost Taylor for good.

Taylor's moist breath against Will's ear was sending a confusingly erotic message, his body hot and sweaty—but Christ, he was thin. Will could feel—could practically count— ribs, the hard links of spine, the ridges of scapula in Taylor's fleshless back. And it scared him; his hold changed instinctively from lock to hug.

"You crazy bastard," he muttered into Taylor's hair.

Taylor struggled again, and this time Will let him go. Taylor got up, not looking at Will, not speaking, walking unsteadily, but with a peculiar dignity, over to the tent.

Watching him, Will opened his mouth, then shut it. Why the hell would he apologize? Taylor had jumped *him*. He watched, scowling, as Taylor crawled inside the tent, rolled out his sleeping bag onto the air mattress Will had remembered to set up for him, pulled his boots off, and climbed into the bag, pulling the flap over his head—like something going back into its shell.

This is stupid, Will thought. We neither of us want this. But what he said was, "Sweet dreams to you too."

Taylor said nothing.

About the Author

Author of nearly ninety titles of classic Male/Male fiction featuring twisty mystery, kick-ass adventure, and unapologetic man-on-man romance, JOSH LANYON'S work has been translated into eleven languages. Her FBI thriller *Fair Game* was the first Male/Male title to be published by Harlequin Mondadori, then the largest romance publisher in Italy. *Stranger on the Shore* (Harper Collins Italia) was the first M/M title to be published in print. In 2016 *Fatal Shadows* placed #5 in Japan's annual Boy Love novel list (the first and only title by a foreign author to place on the list). The Adrien English series was awarded the All-Time Favorite Couple by the Goodreads M/M Romance Group. In 2019, *Fatal Shadows* became the first LGBTQ mobile game created by *Moments: Choose Your Story*.

She is an EPIC Award winner, a four-time Lambda Literary Award finalist (twice for Gay Mystery), an Edgar nominee, and the first ever recipient of the Goodreads All-Time Favorite M/M Author award.

Josh is married and lives in Southern California.

Find other Josh Lanyon titles at www.joshlanyon.com

Follow Josh on Twitter, Facebook, Goodreads, Instagram and Tumblr.

For extras and exclusives, join Josh on Patreon.

ALSO BY JOSH LANYON

NOVELS

The ADRIEN ENGLISH Mysteries

Fatal Shadows • A Dangerous Thing • The Hell You Say
Death of a Pirate King • The Dark Tide
Stranger Things Have Happened • So This is Christmas •

The HOLMES & MORIARITY Mysteries

Somebody Killed His Editor • All She Wrote
The Boy with the Painful Tattoo • In Other Words...Murder

The ALL'S FAIR Series

Fair Game • Fair Play • Fair Chance

The ART OF MURDER Series

The Mermaid Murders •The Monet Murders
The Magician Murders • The Monuments Men Murders
The Movie-Town Murders

BEDKNOBS AND BROOMSTICKS

Mainly by Moonlight • I Buried a Witch
Bell, Book and Scandal

The SECRETS AND SCRABBLE Series

Murder at Pirate's Cove • Secret at Skull House
Mystery at the Masquerade • Scandal at the Salty Dog
Body at Buccaneer's Bay

OTHER NOVELS

This Rough Magic • The Ghost Wore Yellow Socks
Mexican Heat (with Laura Baumbach) • Strange Fortune
Come Unto These Yellow Sands • Stranger on the Shore
Winter Kill • Jefferson Blythe, Esquire
Murder in Pastel • The Curse of the Blue Scarab
The Ghost Had an Early Check-out
Murder Takes the High Road • Séance on a Summer's Night
Hide and Seek

NOVELLAS

The DANGEROUS GROUND Series

Dangerous Ground • Old Poison • Blood Heat
Dead Run • Kick Start • Blind Side

OTHER NOVELLAS

Cards on the Table • The Dark Farewell • The Dark Horse
The Darkling Thrush • The Dickens with Love
I Spy Something Bloody • I Spy Something Wicked
I Spy Something Christmas • In a Dark Wood
The Parting Glass • Snowball in Hell • Mummy Dearest
Don't Look Back • A Ghost of a Chance
Lovers and Other Strangers • Out of the Blue
A Vintage Affair • Lone Star (in Men Under the Mistletoe)
Green Glass Beads (in Irregulars) • Blood Red Butterfly
Everything I Know • Baby, It's Cold (in Comfort and Joy)
A Case of Christmas • Murder Between the Pages
Slay Ride • Stranger in the House

SHORT STORIES

A Limited Engagement • The French Have a Word for It

In Sunshine or In Shadow • Until We Meet Once More

Icecapade (in His for the Holidays) • Perfect Day

Heart Trouble • Other People's Weddings (Petit Mort)

Slings and Arrows (Petit Mort)

Sort of Stranger Than Fiction (Petit Mort)

Critic's Choice (Petit Mort) • Just Desserts (Petit Mort)

In Plain Sight • Wedding Favors • Wizard's Moon

Fade to Black • Night Watch • Plenty of Fish

Halloween is Murder • The Boy Next Door

Requiem for Mr. Busybody

COLLECTIONS

Short Stories (Vol. 1) • Sweet Spot (the Petit Morts)

Merry Christmas, Darling (Holiday Codas)

Christmas Waltz (Holiday Codas 2) • I Spy...Three Novellas

Dangerous Ground The Complete Series

Dark Horse, White Knight (Two Novellas)

The Adrien English Mysteries Box Set

The Adrien English Mysteries Box Set 2

Male/Male Mystery & Suspense Box Set

Partners in Crime (Three Classic Gay Mystery Novels)

All's Fair Complete Collection

Shadows Left Behind: An Historical Mysteries Box Set